THE OFFICIAL SCRAPBOOK

THE OFFICIAL SCRAPBOOK

Adapted from and inspired by the screenplay
The Sisterhood of the Traveling Pants
by Delia Ephron and Elizabeth Chandler

Based on the novel
The Sisterhood of the Traveling Pants
by Ann Brashares

Delacorte Press

Published by Delacorte Press, an imprint of Random House
Children's Books, a division of Random House, Inc.
New York

ISBN: 0-553-37607-1

www.sisterhoodcentral.com
www.randomhouse.com/teens
www.sisterhoodofthetravelingpants.com

PRINTED IN THE UNITED STATES OF AMERICA

April 2005

10 9 8 7 6 5 4 3 2 1

INTRODUCTION

Once upon a time, there was a movie about a pair of pants. . . .

This is a book about that movie.

The Sisterhood of the Traveling Pants, based on the internationally bestselling novel of the same name, introduces us to four lifelong best friends: Bridget, Carmen, Lena, and Tibby.

On a last shopping trip together before parting ways for the first time in their sixteen years, the foursome finds a pair of thrift-shop jeans that—amazingly, astoundingly, maybe even magically—fits each girl perfectly. They decide to use these Pants as a way of keeping in touch over the summer months ahead. Each of them wears the Pants for one week to see what luck the Pants will bring before sending them on to the next girl. Though miles and worlds apart, the four friends experience life, love, and loss together in a summer they'll never forget.

It all adds up to a film *you'll* never want to forget. This photo-packed movie scrapbook will help you remember all your favorite moments, as well as showing you all sorts of behind-the-scenes info, secrets, and trivia about the making of the film.

Now put on your favorite pair of jeans, settle in, and read on. . . .

Contents

A Brief History of Pants, Part 1 1

Seeing Stars: Meet the Girls Who Wear the Pants 9
    . . . And Their Supporting Cast Members 18

In Their Own Words, Part 1 28

A Peek Behind the Scenes:
    Production Secrets Revealed! 33

A Brief History of Pants, Part 2 37

Gotta Love 'Em 44

In Their Own Words, Part 2 48

Production Diary: How We Made It Happen,
    by Christine Sacani, Line Producer 58

A Brief History of Pants, Part 3 64

Quiz: Which Pants Girl Are You? 70

A Peek Behind the Scenes: Film Trivia 74

In Their Own Words, Part 3 78

A Brief History of <u>Pants</u>, part 4 87

A Peek Behind the Scenes: The People Who Made It All
    Happen 99

In Their Own Words, part 4 102

A Brief History of Pants
    (the Regular Kind) 105

In Their Own Words, part 5 108

Quiz: Where in the World . . . ? 112

It's All Greek to Me 115

Production Diary: Stunt
    Coordinating Takes
    On a Whole New Meaning,
    by Lauro Chartrand, Stunt Coordinator 116

In Their Own Words, part 6 120

A Peek Behind the Scenes:
    You Think This Stuff Is Easy?!? 128

By the Numbers 132

A Brief History of <u>Pants</u>, part 5 133

Storyboard artists work out the pacing and action, plotting the sequences of the movie. You'll see a number of storyboards in this book!

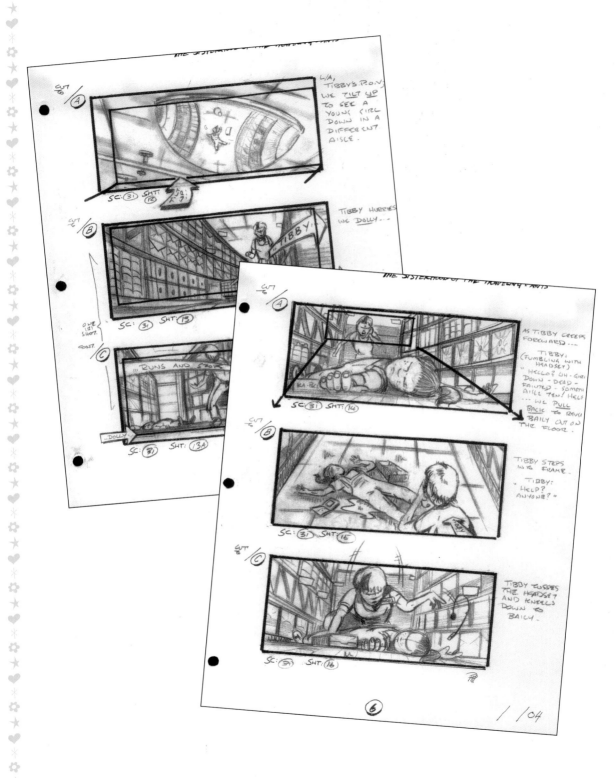

A Brief History of Pants

PART 1

can you guess who's who?

How did it all start? You could say it was when Bridget, Carmen, Lena, and Tibby found the Pants. Then again, you could say it started some sixteen years earlier when four pregnant women met in an aerobics class. Their daughters would end up friends. Best friends—almost like sisters.

But maybe we should let Carmen sum it up:

We'd been a foursome as long as I could remember . . . way before the Pants came into our lives. By then, we'd grown up enough to settle into types.

The summer they all turned sixteen, the girls found themselves heading off in different directions. Lena was flying to Greece to visit her grandparents. Carmen was spending the summer with her father in South Carolina. Bridget was heading to soccer camp in Baja California. Tibby was the only one staying home in Maryland.

Just before they were to part ways for the first time in their lives, the four friends went shopping together and wandered into a thrift store. That was where they found the Pants.

Lena was looking for sundresses to wear in Greece. Conservative sundresses, of course—that was the only kind she wore. As the others poked around waiting for her to finish and lazily rehashing their summer plans, Tibby came across a tray of silver studs.

"Pierce alert!" Carmen cried.

Bridget. the athlete.

Tibby. the rebel.

Lena. the beauty.

And me. Carmen. the writer. Maybe that's what kept us so close all those years—that together. it was as if we formed one single. complete person.

Bridget marched over, mock-stern. "Sorry, young lady," she told Tibby. "No more holes. No more studs."

In a playful attempt to distract Tibby, Carmen grabbed a pair of jeans at random and tossed them her way. "Make her try these on."

They were just ordinary jeans. Well worn, faded, even a little shabby. Little did they know that those jeans were about to change them all forever.

Despite Tibby's protests, she soon had the jeans on. When she stepped out of the dressing room, her friends' jaws dropped.

"My god!" Bridget cried, speaking for all of them. "Tibby, you're a babe!"

Isn't this cute?

Shut up!

It was true. The jeans fit Tibby so perfectly it was as if they'd been made for her, molded specifically for the distinctive curves of her body. Unimpressed, Tibby stripped them off and flung them toward Lena, insisting that she try them.

Some might call it a miracle. Some might prefer the term *coincidence*. But those same jeans that fit Tibby so perfectly fit Lena just as well. As the girls soon discovered, they also fit three-inches-taller Bridget. And shorter, curvy Carmen.

They all realized that something special was happening. Maybe even something life-changing. Carmen saw it as a sign. "Don't you see?" she insisted. "These Pants are trying to tell us something."

Late that night they gathered in the deserted aerobics studio where their mothers had met all those years ago. They lit candles and laid out the food they'd brought. Then they sat in a circle with the Pants in the middle. Carmen picked them up first.

"We are gathered here to honor a gift that has been sent to us," she intoned. "I propose that they belong to us equally, and that this summer they will travel among us, linking our hearts and our spirits, though we be far away from each other."

Bridget spoke next. "Tonight we are the Sisters of the Pantalones!"

Being the practical one of the group, Lena pointed out that every Sisterhood needed rules. Before long the Manifesto of the Pants was written.

Some of the rules were practical: "Each sister keeps them for one week, then passes them on."

Some were silly: "You must never pick your nose while wearing the Pants."

Others were, perhaps, a bit questionable: "You must never wash the Pants."

But there they were. The girls all promised to obey the Manifesto. And each of them knew the truth of the final rule: "Pants equal love. Love your pals, love yourself."

Family!

Lena had the Pants first, since she was traveling the farthest. They were packed safely in her bag as she perched awkwardly on the back of a slow-moving don-key, making her way along a cliffside path on her way to her grandparents' home in Santorini.

I'm really here...

Being in Greece was a little overwhelming. It wasn't helping matters any that her grandfather, Papou, had been virtually silent the whole way up the cliff. Lena wasn't sure what to say to him. She wasn't even sure if he spoke English.

It was almost a relief to arrive at the Kaligaris Café, her family's homey restaurant. Her grandmother, Yia-Yia, grabbed her, smothering her in a hug as countless other strangers — Lena's cousins — pressed forward to welcome her to Santorini. 💕

Meanwhile, Bridget arrived at soccer camp in Baja California. Jazzed up and eager to get started, she had trouble standing still as the head counselor, Donna, divided the girls into teams.

As Bridget waited for her assignment, one of the team coaches suddenly caught her eye. "Who's that?" Bridget asked her bunk mates, Diana and Olivia.

Ooof! . . . .

Olivia knew who Bridget meant right away. "Don't even think about it," she warned. "It's against the rules to have flings with the coaches."

But rules had never meant much to Bridget, especially since her mother had died. She continued to stare at the Green coach even as she was assigned to the Red team. Bridget had arrived at camp with the goals of having fun and improving her game.

Now she had another goal. ✮

Eric Richman.

Seeing Stars:
Meet the Girls Who Wear the Pants...

Something magical's about to happen . . . .

Here's your chance for a close-up look at the talented actresses who bring <u>sisterhood</u> to life.

Alexis Bledel "Lena"

Recent Résumé

You probably know Alexis best as Rory Gilmore, the smart, savvy teen daughter of a free-spirited single mother, on the WB's critically acclaimed series *The Gilmore Girls*.

History

Alexis began her acting career appearing in community theater in her hometown, Houston. She also modeled in New York City during her school breaks. Before winning the role on *The Gilmore Girls*, Alexis attended NYU Film School to study writing and directing. In 2002 she made her feature film debut, costarring with Ben Kingsley, William Hurt, Sissy Spacek, and Jonathan Jackson in *Tuck Everlasting*.

Awards and Honors

Her portrayal of Rory earned Alexis the 2002 Family Friendly Forum Award for Best Actress in a Drama, as well as nominations for Choice Actress in a Drama at the 2002, 2003, and 2004 Teen Choice Awards. The series was named 2001's Outstanding New Program by the Television Critics Association.

What's Next?

Alexis will be seen next in the independent film *Orphan King* by writer-director Andrew Wilder, as well as *Bride and Prejudice*, a Bollywood musical version of Jane Austen's *Pride and Prejudice*.

Also known as: Len; Lenny.

Special talent: Art.

Likes: Painting and sketching; looking for the meaning of things; hanging out with her friends; Kostos.

Dislikes: People who judge on appearances; too-tight clothes; being put on the spot; donkeys (at first, anyway).

Fashion sense: Classic, comfortable, and definitely not too revealing.

Family: Back home, she lives with her mother and father. In Greece, she has her grandmother Yia-Yia, grandfather Papou, and way too many cousins to name.

Classic Lena quote: *"I'm not wearing a bikini!"*

So many things to draw.

Alexis will also be a part of the ensemble cast of the Robert Rodriguez film *Sin City*, which also stars Bruce Willis, Josh Hartnett, Rosario Dawson, and Brittany Murphy.

Meet Lena Kaligaris

Lena is known as the beauty of the group—much to her own dismay. She'd prefer that people appreciate her for her art. If they have to notice her at all, that is.

Good-bye Greece.

What a way to spend the summer.

Amber Tamblyn "Tibby"

Recent Résumé

Amber is the star of the hit
TV series *Joan of Arcadia*,
playing the title character,
an ordinary young woman who
has conversations with God.

History

A California girl, Amber gained fame as Emily Quartermaine
on the long-running soap *General Hospital*. What was originally going to be a few months' work turned into a seven-year
stint as she won viewers' hearts and critical acclaim. Since
then she has appeared on many other TV series, including
*Buffy the Vampire Slayer, The Twilight Zone, Boston Public, CSI:
Miami,* and *Without a Trace.* On the big screen, Amber
appeared in the film *The Ring.*

Awards and Honors

Can we go soon?

Amber's work on *Joan of Arcadia* earned
her both Emmy and Golden Globe nom-
inations for Best Actress in a Leading
Role—Drama Series. In her *General
Hospital* days Amber won two consecu-
tive *Hollywood Reporter* Young Star
Awards for Best Young Actress in a
Daytime Series.

Personal Notes

Amber's father is veteran actor Russ Tamblyn (*West Side Story*). She considers him the guiding light for her success. Amber is also a published poet.

Meet Tibby Rollins

Tibby is a rebel with a cause: recording the stupidity of the world in her latest "suckumentary" video. She's the cynic of the group, with a dark sense of humor and a talent for looking on the dark side of life through the lens of her video camera. But is that lens her tool—or her buffer against the world?

The perfect subject for my suckumentary.

Babysitting—how fun.

Also known as: Tib; Tibberon; Drama Queen. The name on her birth certificate is Tabitha Tomko-Rollins, but these days she mostly just goes by Tibby Rollins.

Special talent: Cinematography.

Likes: Her video camera; bacon pizza; exploring the stupid side of life; the three least-lame friends in the world.

Dislikes: Babysitting; stupid people; Duncan Howe.

Fashion sense: Funky vintage stuff—lots of black. Her nose ring clashes with her Wallman's uniform, but that's okay. Tibby doesn't mind clashing.

Family: A few years ago Tibby's ex-hippie parents decided to give the yuppie thing a try, which means they went out and got "real" jobs, expensive cars . . . and two new young siblings for Tibby.

Classic Tibby quote: "Can pizza give you a hangover?"

America Ferrera
"Carmen"

Where are you, Dad?

Recent Résumé

America made a big splash in her feature film debut, *Real Women Have Curves*, on HBO.

History

America is the youngest of her Honduran parents' six kids. She's a natural performer who started acting in school plays and landed her first show-biz job on the Disney Channel as a cheerleader in 2002's *Gotta Kick It Up*. Since then she has been involved in a variety of other film and TV projects and has appeared in episodes of *CSI* and *Touched by an Angel*.

Awards and Honors

America and her *Real Women* costar, Lupe Ontiveros, won a Special Jury Prize for Acting at the Sundance Film Festival. America was also nominated for an Independent Spirit Award for Best Debut Performance.

What's Next?

America's upcoming film projects include *How the Garcia Girls Spent Their Summer* and the skateboarding movie *Lords of Dogtown*. As if that wasn't enough to keep her busy, she is also studying international relations at the University of Southern California.

Talking with a friend.

Also known as: Carma; Car; Carmabelle; Carmencita (only by her mom); Pumpkin (only by her dad).

Special talents: Writing; Spanish (she is bilingual, thanks to her Puerto Rican mother).

Likes: Her big butt; writing; her three best friends; bright colors (both literally and figuratively speaking).

Dislikes: Her big butt; confrontation; surprises; feeling like the Wicked Stepdaughter.

Fashion sense: Colorful, funky, and fun.

Family: Divorce City. Carmen lives with her mother in Maryland. She sees her father in South Carolina a few times per year. It's not ideal, but it works. That is, until the Rodmans enter her life.

Classic Carmen quote: "There's no way pants that fit all of you are going to fit all of this."

Please don't make me wear this.

Meet Carmen Lowell

Carmen just might be the glue that holds the Sisterhood together. Quick to laugh and quick to cry, she's perceptive, kindhearted, and patient. Maybe a little *too* patient at times.

Blake Lively
"Bridget"

Recent Résumé

Believe it or not, *Sisterhood* is Blake's big-screen debut!

History

Blake was born into a showbiz family in Tarzana, California. Her mother is a talent manager and her father is actor-director Ernie Lively, who also appears in *Sisterhood* as Bridget's father. Blake's four siblings are all actors, too. At the age of ten Blake played the Tooth Fairy in *Sandman*, a film directed by her father.

Awards and Honors

None to report yet—but give her time!

What's Next?

After completing filming on *The Sisterhood of the Traveling Pants*, Blake returned to high school for her senior year. A true all-American teenager, she stays busy juggling duties as class president and cheerleader as well as performing with her national championship show choir.

I like what I see.

Saddest of days.

Meet Bridget Vreeland

Bridget is the bright, bold, big-hearted athlete of the group. It's hard not to like someone like Bridget—she grabs life by the hand and drags it along behind her. Of course, some might say that's because she's afraid to slow down. . . .

Also known as: Bee; Bee-Bee; Bridge; Vreeland.

Special talents: Soccer and other sports; great people skills (most of the time).

Likes: Sports, sports, and more sports. She also loves any kind of challenge. Oh, and her three best pals, of course.

Dislikes: Sitting still; being sad.

Fashion sense: Practical and, yes, sporty.

Family: Since her mom's death, Bridget and her father do their best to keep each other company.

Classic Bridget quote: "What can I say? I'm obsessed."

Soccer star!

...And Their Supporting Cast Members

The Sisterhood of the Traveling Pants wouldn't be the same without the support of these outstanding actors.

Jenna Boyd "Bailey"

Jenna proves that big things come in small packages. This Texas girl has been modeling since age two and acting almost as long. Her first TV appearance was on *The Barney Show*. Jenna has been keeping very busy over the past couple of years shooting a variety of feature films, including *The Missing*.

Jenna's other passion is figure skating. She has been skating for eight years and has won numerous awards in competition. When she's not acting or skating, Jenna is fulfilling her duties as student council president and founder of her spy club.

Seeing beneath it all.

Meet Bailey Graffman

Wise (and obnoxious) beyond her years, twelve-year-old Bailey falls into Tibby's life—literally—and changes it forever.

Things to know about Bailey: She has leukemia, but she's not going to let a little thing like that keep her down. She has a real talent for connecting with people—all people. Even Tibby.

Classic Bailey quote: "Maybe the truth is, there is a little bit of the pathetic in all of us."

This is my country.

Michael Rady
"Kostos"

A fresh new face in film acting: *Sisterhood* marks Michael's first major motion picture appearance. But it almost certainly won't be his last!

Hailing from Philadelphia, Michael sings; surfs; snowboards; speaks Italian; plays piano, guitar, and drums; ice-skates; rollerblades; and enjoys many other sports. He has experience as a bartender and is an Eagle Scout. Now, that's well-rounded!

Meet Kostos Dounas

Tall, dark, and handsome, Kostos is enough to make most girls drool. But Lena isn't sure he's worth the trouble of defying her family . . . until the Pants give her the strength to decide what she really wants.

Things to know about Kostos: Fluent in English and Greek, he lived with his parents in Chicago until they died when he was a young boy. He attends the university in Athens. During the summer, he works on his grandfather's fishing fleet in Santorini.

Classic Kostos quote: "No one sits near a smelly fish market unless they're waiting for someone."

Who is that blond chick?

Mike Vogel
"Eric"

Philly native Eric spent a year commuting to New York City for auditions. But when he landed a recurring role as Dean on the hit sitcom *Grounded for Life*, he packed up and headed to Los Angeles, where he now lives.

Eric's a dog lover and has two pugs. He recently wrapped production on the independent film *Havoc*, as well as *Supercross* and *Rumor Has It* with Jennifer Aniston and Kevin Costner.

Meet Eric Richman

From the first time she lays eyes on him, Bridget is smitten with blond, handsome, and older Eric, one of the coaches at soccer camp.

Things to know about Eric: A student at Columbia University, Eric is intense about everything. Soccer. Running. His job at the camp. And, ultimately, his feelings for Bridget.

Classic Eric quote: "The endorphins don't suck either."

Leonardo Nam
"Brian McBrian"

The Dragon Master.

Leonardo was born in Argentina. When he was a young boy his family moved to Sydney, Australia. He studied architecture at the University of New South Wales before moving to New York City to pursue an acting career. He now splits his time between NYC and L.A.

Leonardo has trained at the New York Shakespeare Festival/Public Theatre and the Actors Lab in Sydney. His other film credits include *Meridian, Hacks,* and *The Perfect Score*.

Meet Brian McBrian

King of the Quik-Mart Dragon Master game. He starts off as one of the subjects of Tibby's suckumentary but soon turns into something more: a friend.

Things to know about Brian: February 12 — the memorable date when he reached Round 28 on Dragon Master. At first Tibby thinks that's all there is to Brian. But when he stands by Bailey in her darkest hour, she realizes that maybe there are at least twenty-eight levels to him, too.

Classic Brian quote: "Only one person's ever made it all the way to Round Twenty-eight on this machine."

Bradley Whitford
"Al"

A native of Wisconsin, Bradley studied theater and English literature at Wesleyan University and attended the Juilliard Theater Center in New York City. His big-screen credits include *Scent of a Woman, Billy Madison, Philadelphia, The Client, Presumed Innocent,* and *Adventures in Babysitting,* among many others. He's best known for playing the sarcastic yet vulnerable Josh Lyman on *The West Wing,* for which he earned a 2001 Emmy Award as well as Golden Globe nominations in 2000, 2001, and 2002.

Bradley is married to *Malcolm in the Middle* star Jane Kaczmarek. They live in Los Angeles and have three children.

Meet Al Lowell

Carmen's father loves her — just as he does his "new" family, the Rodmans. Carmen is his flesh and blood, now and always.

Isn't this great?

Things to know about Al: He likes to avoid conflict at all costs. But he's crazy about Carmen, even if he doesn't always know how to show it.

Classic Al quote: "You'll see—it'll be perfect."

Nancy Travis
"Lydia"

I do.

Nancy was born in New York and grew up in Baltimore and Boston. She studied drama at New York University. She has appeared in numerous plays, movies, and TV shows. Her film credits include *Three Men and a Baby*, *Air America*, *Internal Affairs*, and *So I Married an Ax Murderer*. On TV she starred opposite Ted Danson in the hit TV comedy series *Becker*. She also starred in the Stephen King miniseries *Rose Red*.

Rachel Ticotin
(Carmen's mom)

Mom and daughter.

Born and raised in New York City, Rachel started her career as a dancer with the Ballet Hispanico of New York when she was twelve years old! Among the most recent entries in Rachel's long list of cinematic accomplishments are her roles in *Man on Fire* with Denzel Washington and Dakota Fanning and in *Something's Gotta Give*. And Rachel supplied the voice for Captain Maria Chavez on the animated series *Gargoyles*.

Happy Birthday!

A beat, as the Girls stare at the Pants...   *

                                                        CUT TO:

10   EXT. STREET - BETHESDA - NIGHT

Each wearing a backpack, and Carmen carrying the Pants, the   *
Girls head down a dimly lit, deserted street.   *

                    TIBBY   *
          This is crazy.   *

                    CARMEN   *
          Look, something happened today that   *
          none of us can explain. We can't   *
          just *ignore* that.   *

                    TIBBY   *
          Why not?   *

                    CARMEN   *
          Because it's got to be a sign.   *
          Don't you see? These Pants are   *
          trying to tell us something.   *

They turn into an alley.   *

                                                   CUT TO:

11   EXT. ALLEY - NIGHT

As the Girls head into the dark alley, Tibby grabs the Pants   *
from Carmen and puts them dramatically to her ear.   *

                    TIBBY   *
          Wait, I hear it. They're saying...   *
          "Don't walk into deserted alleyways   *
          at night."   *

Carmen grabs the Pants back.   *

                    CARMEN   *
          Ha ha, Tib. Just keep watch.   *

Tibby rolls her eyes and stands look-out while Carmen, Lena,   *
and Bridget approach the back of an old building. Bridget
starts climbing onto a dumpster.   *

                    BRIDGET   *
        All I know is, they make every one *
        of our butts look good. That's *
        enough for me. *

                    LENA *
          (practical as always) *
        Maybe there's Lycra in them. A *
        high enough content would *
        definitely allow them to change *
        shape-- *

She stops as she sees Bridget fearlessly makes a dangerous *
leap to grab the railing of a nearby fire escape. Lena
stifles a scream as Bridget hangs precariously above them, *
but in an instant Bridget has hoisted herself up to the
platform. She grins down at the girls as if oblivious to the
risks she has just taken and sends down the fire escape *
ladder for them to climb. Carmen looks at Lena. *

                  CARMEN *
        I'm telling you, there's something *
        more going on here than Lycra. *

She starts up the fire escape ladder, while Bridget starts to *
jimmy a second-story door lock.

                                 CUT TO:

12   INT. SMALL DANCE STUDIO - NIGHT

The girls break into the room, their FLASHLIGHTS sweeping
across the mirrored walls...until we realize we're in the
same dance studio where their mothers had aerobics class.

A MONTAGE, as the Girls dump out their backpacks and set up.
CANDLES are arranged on the floor; JUNK FOOD is laid out in
piles; the JEANS are placed in the center of the makeshift
shrine; the FLASHLIGHTS are turned off as Bridget starts
lighting the candles, filling the room with a glow.

The Girls sit in a circle. Carmen solemnly crosses herself.

                  CARMEN
        In the name of the Father...

                  TIBBY
      Here we go.

                  BRIDGET
      Car, this isn't church.   *

                    CARMEN
          Well, it's still a sacred place.
          This is where our moms met and--

She catches herself with a guilty glance at Bridget, who
pretends not to be affected in the least as she continues to
light candles.

                    CARMEN
               (picking up the Jeans)
          Anyway, we are gathered here to
          honor a gift that has been sent to
          us.

                    TIBBY
          So, why'd we have to pay for 'em,
          then?

                    LENA
          Tib, can we just go with this
          please?

                    CARMEN
               (resuming her speech)
          Today, on the eve of our
          separation, magic has come to us in
          a pair of Pants.

She passes the Jeans around the circle.

                    CARMEN
          I propose that they belong to us
          equally, and that this summer they
          will travel among us, linking our
          hearts and our spirits, though we
          be far away from each other.

Bridget lights the last candle as she intones:

                    BRIDGET
          Tonight we are the Sisters of the
          Pants.

She watches the match burn close to her fingers, until Lena
blows it out just before it burns her. Bridget laughs.

                    LENA
          We need rules. Every Sisterhood
          has rules.

                    CARMEN
          A "manifesto." Good point.

In Their Own Words

PART 1

Getting it right with director Ken Kwapis.

Wonder what it's like to be involved with the making of a film like <u>sisterhood</u>? Now you can hear all about it from the people who were there from start to finish.

Magic from the Start

When Debra Martin Chase read Ann Brashares's bestselling novel *The Sisterhood of the Traveling Pants*, she fell in love. "I laughed, I cried, I couldn't put it down," she says.

While Chase is a Disney-based producer, it was Warner Bros. that was interested in making the picture and acquired the rights to the book. The studio teamed Chase with Warner Bros.–based producer Denise Di Novi.

As synchronicity would have it, when they read the novel, Andrew Kosove and Broderick Johnson, the copresidents of Alcon Entertainment, were also determined to make the movie. The executives lobbied their distribution partner, Warner Bros., which agreed that Alcon would be the studio to produce *The Sisterhood of the Traveling Pants*.

Part of what appealed to Kosove was that "*The Sisterhood of the Traveling Pants* is intelligent. It's also funny in places, and light and charming, but it deals with real issues that teenagers can relate to."

"It was love at first read," adds Johnson. "It was very touching and felt very real." And thus Kosove, Johnson, Chase, and Di Novi joined forces to produce the movie.

Direct Effect

When Chase met with Ken Kwapis for the first time, she had high expectations. The director, best known for his slate of groundbreaking television comedies, blew the producer away. "In great detail, Ken proceeded to talk about each character and [her] friendships with such complete understanding," she recalls. "He walked out the door and I said to myself, 'This is the guy.' And it's been one of the most wonderful partnerships. I can't imagine anybody else doing it."

Direction. direction. direction.

When he first read the script, what struck Kwapis was that "the four stories were so different and the characters were different types, and yet I was able to identify with them equally." It reminded him of one of his favorite films, George Lucas's *American Graffiti*.

"Here is a picture with four very different characters with whom an audience could identify because they represent different parts of all of us," Kwapis says. "Every one of us is shy and awkward, like Lena. Every one of us at least dreams of being impulsive and active, like Bridget. Every one of us has a sarcastic, rebellious side, like Tibby. Every one of us at least yearns to be passionate and expressive, like Carmen, even if we aren't all the time."

Rave Reviews for Ken Kwapis

Jenna Boyd describes the director as "young-person friendly. Ken's more playful and it seems like he's worked with a lot of other kid actors."

"Ken is a miracle," agrees Amber Tamblyn. "He was very quiet at the beginning and I wasn't sure of him, but he has turned out to be one of the best people I've ever had a chance to work with."

"He asked everything and was curious and he really wanted to tell the story correctly," says Alexis Bledel. "In Greece, he'd give me really subtle notes to change my performance and they made the scenes so much funnier. I would actually crack up before I even did it because I knew it would be funny."

"Ken's commitment and sensitivity are hard to find," America Ferrera says. "He allows himself to be part of the Sisterhood. I had my doubts when I heard that a man would

This is harder than it looks.

be directing the movie, but when I met Ken, I just knew that nobody but him could direct it. Because he understood the sensitivity, and what he didn't understand, he wasn't afraid to ask questions and let us play and let us put ourselves into it. He knew that until it was real to us, it wouldn't be real to anybody else."

A Peek Behind the Scenes:
Production Secrets Revealed!

capturing the vision.

Anyone who's ever seen one of those "Making Of" specials on TV knows that filmmakers are masters of illusion, ingenuity, and special effects. Read on for the inside scoop on some of the tricks of the trade that went into making <u>The Sisterhood of the Traveling Pants</u>.

Shadow Trouble

The Pants Manifesto scene was filmed by placing the camera on a 360-degree dolly track around the girls. Unfortunately, it was virtually impossible for the camera to complete the circle around them without its own shadow being visible at some point in the scene (as the camera passed in front of the lights). Luckily, the visual effects people came to the rescue and "erased" the shadow from the shot.

Forming the sisterhood.

Unconventional "Action"

Director Ken Kwapis never uses the traditional film command "Action!" to begin the actors' performance on set. Instead he says, "Quiet, please, and um, uh, g'ahead." This method is much more relaxed and allows the actors to begin at their own pace. However, he did get teased about it—someone even printed up bright orange T-shirts quoting him and handed them out to the crew!

Go Play Outside

Remember the scene in which Tibby and Bailey lie out in the park staring up at a sky full of stars and talking about life and death? Well, in reality that scene was shot *inside* on a soundstage. Parts of the movie were shot in and around Vancouver, British Columbia, Canada, and shooting on the soundstage saved the actors and the crew from having to work outside in the cold, cold, cold Canadian night.

Losing a Location

Less than a week before shooting was to begin, the people who owned the original choice of location for "Tibby's house" decided they didn't want a film crew inside their home after all. Sound like a serious problem? Not for these filmmakers! They quickly found a new location for the living room scenes and built Tibby's bedroom on a soundstage.

Just Add Water

Remember that gorgeous green grassy soccer field? Believe it or not, those scenes were shot in a desert in Cache Creek, Canada! (Yes, Canada has deserts!) The crew actually grew grass there. But naturally, in the middle of a desert, there was no water. So the crew put up a huge green screen in Cache Creek behind where they shot the soccer scenes and then shot footage of the ocean in Mexico. Presto—thanks to the talented visual effects people, the two shots became one!

Swimming in Canada?

One dramatic moment in the film happens when Kostos saves Lena from drowning. However, it proved too complicated to mount an underwater shooting unit in Greece for that scene. So while the above-the-water action was shot on location, the

The harbor.

underwater sequence was filmed in a tank in Vancouver that is normally used for dive research. And go figure—the water in the tank in Canada was much warmer than the harbor in Greece.

Hair Today, Gone Tomorrow

Both Alexis Bledel and Blake Lively had extensions added to their already long and beautiful hair. Lena needed dark, thick, wavy hair; Bridget needed gorgeous waist-length blond hair. The hair extensions were put in in Los Angeles but needed to be tightened and maintained every two weeks in Vancouver. Alexis had hers removed at three a.m. on the day she finished filming because she had to start work on her TV show, *The Gilmore Girls*, the next day. However, Blake loved hers so much that she left them in for two months after filming!

Meanwhile, Amber Tamblyn added her own blue streak to Tibby's hair. She was scheduled to do a photo shoot for a magazine the day after she finished shooting and begin filming *Joan of Arcadia* a day after that, so she had to get her hair back to normal—fast. To accomplish that, she had to bleach out the blue and then redye her hair its original color.

check out those movie dos!

A Brief History of Pants
PART 2

The Pants!

Carmen's only goal for the summer was making up for lost time with her father. She arrived in Charleston, South Carolina, ready to get started. She chattered a mile a minute as they drove away from the airport, until she noticed that they were heading out of the city.

"Where are we going?" she asked.

Al Lowell smiled. "I've got a few surprises for you," he told her. "I moved." A few minutes later, he turned the car into a gated community.

Carmen was surprised. "To a development?" she asked. "You hate developments."

She couldn't believe he hadn't bothered to tell her he'd moved. But his new address was

Home?

the least of the surprises he had in store. Waiting for them at Al's new home were perky blond Lydia Rodman and her two blond children, seventeen-year-old Paul and thirteen-year-old Krista.

Al put his arm around Lydia. "We're getting married," he announced happily, not seeming to notice the shock on Carmen's face. "August twenty-third." ✿

There was a serious lack of surprises in Tibby's life at the moment. It was no surprise that her red Wallman's smock was hideous. Or that her job was incredibly boring. Or even that her boss, Duncan, was a complete and total jerk.

Tibby.

After Duncan reminded Tibby for the ten millionth time to wear her employee headset, she put her pricing gun to her forehead, pretending to shoot herself.

Suddenly there was a crash from the next aisle. When Tibby walked over, she saw a young girl sprawled out on the floor in the middle of a pile of hair-dye kits, unconscious.

Tibby fumbled with her headset. "Hello?" she cried into the mouthpiece. "Uh, girl down—dead, fainted, something. Aisle ten. Help!"

The headset wouldn't work right, so she yanked it off and yelled for help. Then she grabbed the girl's wallet, hoping to find out her identity.

Soon the paramedics arrived. As they carried the girl out on a stretcher, her eyes fluttered open and focused on Tibby. "There's a price tag on your forehead," she mumbled.

Wearing the Pants, Lena sat by the harbor sketching a fishing boat. When the fisherman turned around, she realized he was only about eighteen years old. She couldn't help staring as he peeled off his shirt.

Then he moved out of sight. Lena leaned forward for another glimpse. She teetered . . . and splashed into the harbor! She flailed in the water. But the hem of the Pants was snagged between two

Nah. it's not slimy.

rocks. She struggled to free herself . . . and suddenly felt strong arms wrap around her, yanking her toward the surface. Before she knew what was happening, she was staring up at the gorgeous young guy. He spoke to her in Greek.

"I—I'm sorry," Lena stammered. "I don't understand Greek very well."

He smiled. "We'll have to work on that, won't we?" His name was Kostos Dounas.

"I have to let the small ones go," Kostos said, gesturing to a bucket of fish. "Would you like to help?"

He lent her a shirt, then showed her how to hold the fish by putting her hands on his. Lena was a little breathless at how close they were. She tossed the fish back into the harbor and watched it swim away.

"I—I should go." She was suddenly uncomfortable with the whole situation. "Thanks again for, um, saving my life."

Kostos wanted to see her again: "Taverna Katina," he said. "Saturday night."

"I'm sorry," Lena blurted out. "I can't." She hurried away, not daring to look back. 💜💜

It was another hot day in Baja, and a group of campers was going for a run along the coast. Eric Richman was leading the run, which meant that Bridget was there.

She drew alongside him, matching her strides to his. "Hi," she said.

"Hi," he replied.

They talked as they ran, with Bridget doing her best to get to know him. Eric answered her questions politely but seemed determined to avoid her attempts at flirting.

"Race ya," Bridget dared him after a while. She sprinted ahead.

Eric couldn't resist the challenge. They raced along, neck and neck. Soon they had left the rest of the girls far behind. Finally Eric slowed, dropping onto the sand, breathing hard.

"That's it," he said. "Seven miles."

Bridget flung herself down beside him. They talked some more, and this time Eric seemed a little friendlier. Maybe it was just the endorphins talking, but Bridget didn't care. All she cared about was being there, under the burning Mexican sun, with him. . . .⋆⋆

We could run all day.

That evening Carmen sat down to dinner with her father and the Rodmans. She was still reeling from all the changes in her father's life. Why hadn't he told her?

While they ate, Lydia and Al told Carmen the story of how they'd met. It was something about a wrong number, but Carmen didn't really care. Everything they said seemed to contradict everything she knew—or had thought she knew—about her father. It was all wrong, wrong, wrong.

Later, she called her mother. "I don't blame you for being angry," Carmen's mother soothed her. "It was terrible of him to just spring this on you."

Carmen couldn't help defending her father. "He wanted to surprise me."

"You need to talk to him, Carmencita," her mother said. "*Hablale*. Tell him how you feel. What he did was wrong."

Carmen was so confused and angry she wasn't sure what to think. But the last thing she wanted to do was damage things with Al even more. "You just don't want him to be happy," she accused her mother. "That's why you're blaming him. Look, forget it, okay? This is going to work out great."

Without waiting for a response, she hung up. ✿

In Santorini, Lena prepared to send the Pants to Tibby. She was a little disappointed that nothing much had happened to her while wearing them. Well, other than almost drowning, of course. But that wasn't really the sort of adventure she'd imagined. She wrote a note and tucked it into a pocket, then took the package to the FedEx office.

Then she went to the café. Yia-Yia was doing the laundry and found the T-shirt Lena had borrowed from Kostos.

"Is yours?" she asked, looking confused.

"Actually, no, I—sort of borrowed it," Lena stammered. She explained what had happened. "His name is Kostos Dounas."

Yia-Yia's eyes widened. "Dounas? He's a Dounas?"

With that, she burst into a torrent of Greek, sounding shocked and horrified. Some of Lena's Greek cousins overheard and joined in.

"What's wrong?" Lena cried.

"Never speak of them!" Yia-Yia exclaimed angrily. "Your grandfather would die if he knew this. Promise me you will never see this boy again, or you will break Papou's heart." She grabbed Lena's arms. "You must swear it!"

Lena was horrified and confused. But what could she do?

"I swear," she said. 💙💚

Gotta Love 'Em

Yia-Yia's delicious cooking.

Life might be easier for the Sisterhood if its members never had to interact with anyone outside the group. But that's not how life works—and really, isn't it better that way? Here are a few of the more interesting characters the girls meet.

Yia-Yia and Papou

Lena's Greek grandparents are an odd couple indeed—Papou rarely says a word, while his wife never seems to stop talking. But they share a special bond that Lena learns to understand.

Things to Know About Lena's Grandparents

Papou is eighty-one, quiet, and iron-willed. He has a way with donkeys, but not so much with English (or Greek, for that matter). Luckily his wife, Yia-Yia, talks more than enough for both of them. She is lively, loving, and loquacious. Together, the two of them run the family business, the Kaligaris Café. They hold a grudge against Kostos's grandfather because of a long-ago feud over fish, but Lena helps them overcome the hurts of the past to embrace the promise of the present.

Classic Yia-Yia Quote

"In this life, family is the most precious gift we are given."

Very interesting.

Ahh, my Lena.

Duncan Howe

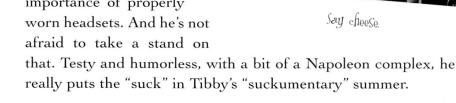

Say cheese.

Tibby's boss at Wallman's takes his job seriously. Very seriously.

Things to Know About Duncan

He believes in the importance of properly worn headsets. And he's not afraid to take a stand on that. Testy and humorless, with a bit of a Napoleon complex, he really puts the "suck" in Tibby's "suckumentary" summer.

Classic Duncan Quote

"I'm afraid our dress code strictly prohibits blue jeans."

Maggie

Come back, Maggie!

Bridget's dog, a lovable but sometimes disobedient golden retriever.

Things to Know About Maggie

She has a taste for Pants— and a knack for timing.

The Rodmans—Lydia, Paul, and Krista

At first Carmen isn't sure she's going to be able to tolerate her instant new stepfamily. Her father's wife-to-be, Lydia, and Lydia's two teenage kids all seem way too blond and perfect for Carmen. But in end she realizes that they're not so perfect after all . . . which is just fine with her.

Things to Know About the Rodmans

Lydia has always dreamed of having the picture-book wedding she missed out on the first time. The two kids have very different ways of dealing with their alcoholic father; Paul visits him regularly, while Krista pretends he doesn't exist.

Classic Rodmans quote

According to Lydia, *"Turns out the place doesn't matter after all. It's who's here that makes it perfect."*

You're all so . . . blond.

In Their Own Words

PART 2

Nice.

Central Casting

"We were looking for really great actresses who felt real," says Andrew Kosove.

"Casting on this was key," says Debra Martin Chase. "We were fortunate to have interest from pretty much every young actress in Hollywood and we met with everybody."

Not only did each young woman cast need to be a terrific actress in her

This pic is on carmen's bulletin board.

own right, she also needed to fit the part. "The readers know this book and the characters so well; we really wanted our choices to embody the essence of each one," says Chase. "Equally important, we needed young women that we felt, and hoped, would bond and truly create the Sisterhood. Without that, there's no movie."

"The four actresses so perfectly embody their roles it's hard for me to imagine anyone else in these parts," says Kwapis. "The truth is, we met a lot of good actresses. But in each case, when we met Amber, America, Alexis, and Blake, the search was over."

All About Amber

Amber Tamblyn was drawn to the project, she says, because of "the friendship [among] the four girls and how realistic the characters were, and the experiences that they had together. So many times I feel like teen films are really based on the drama of the

careful. these are magic pants.

moment, as opposed to the whole story and evolution of the character." While she admits there are very sad moments in the film, she points out there are happy, sweet moments as well. "I don't think being a teenage girl is all about being sad all the time."

The director finds it hard to imagine a better Tibby. "Amber has such a keen intelligence, such a sharp wit and cynical point of view on things. It's not all edge. She's so full of heart and she was able to bring so many different layers to the part."

Denise Di Novi says, "Tibby has a wisdom beyond her years and a great sense of humor. Amber delivers all those qualities. She's a brilliant young actress with enormous charisma."

"It's effortless and just flows from her," adds Chase. "She's so funny, and so politically aware." But then, as the producer points out, "Her dad is Russ Tamblyn, the great actor in one of the most beloved classics of all time (*West Side Story*), and her godfathers are Dennis Hopper and Neil Young."

Alexis: A Face for the Ages

Kwapis suggests that if Alexis Bledel had been an actress in the 1920s, she would have been one of the greatest silent film stars. "She has an amazing ability to express character through gesture, nuance, and facial expression. She's an extraordinary beauty, but

What will these bring me?

her face also seems to exist a little out of time. When I photographed her, I thought of the great female silent stars." In Lena's story in particular, Kwapis wanted to have physical comedy. "I had silent cinema in mind. I was thinking of people like Buster Keaton, and Alexis has an amazing ability to do delicate physical comedy and make it feel incredibly natural and still — and she can really execute a pratfall."

"With her startling beauty and magnificent eyes," says Chase, "I have no doubt that Alexis has spent her whole life having people stare at her. And yet inside she is this wonderfully smart, funny, kind, and delightful person. I know she identifies with Lena and, on a fundamental level, she embodies the character."

Rock On, America

Unafraid to speak her mind, "Carmen is the rock character," says Denise Di Novi. "She's the one who always says what she thinks and feels and what everybody wishes they could say."

Carmen is the secretary and historian of the group, who narrates the story.

You want to wear them again?

"It's impossible to imagine anyone better than America," Kwapis says, "because among other things, she's literary. America is a voracious reader. She's a great combination of somebody so passionate, emotional, and thoughtful."

Blake's Big Break

The hardest character to cast was Bridget. "Who'd have thought that sort of vibrant, attractive, energetic, all-American blond, blue-eyed girl would be hard to find in Southern California?" muses Chase. "We literally saw every attractive, blond, athletically built actress in the broadest age range. But a lot of teenagers blessed with those gifts and attributes haven't really focused on developing their acting—they're coasting on their looks and presence."

When Blake Lively entered her audition, the director turned over her head shot to check her résumé. On the back of her photo was nothing. Blank. No previous work whatsoever. "I thought it was a joke," says Chase.

Kwapis says he turned to the casting directors and felt like saying, "How could you bring in someone who has no experience—this is a lead role in a major motion picture!" He's glad he didn't. Blake read, and Kwapis was amazed. "I think she read three scenes and when she left, I turned to the casting director and said, 'Bridget just walked

Home is where the Pants are.

out of the room.' It was hard to imagine — I don't think Blake's ever had a paying acting job in her life. But she's absolutely right for the part. And she grew into it so wonderfully."

Her costars found it fun to watch Blake. "She's the youngest of us," says Amber Tamblyn, "and this is her first big thing and we're all so excited for her. It feels like I've been learning a lot from her, and if this is her first thing, well, she's a natural."

The youngest child in a show business family, Blake grew up on film sets. Her four brothers and sisters are actors, as is her father, Ernie Lively, who was cast to play Bridget's father in *The Sisterhood of the Traveling Pants*. "It was wonderful, but really weird," Blake says about acting with her real-life dad. "We have such a close relationship, but we're supposed to be really distant in the movie." As soon as the director called "Cut!" father and daughter would hold hands. "It was definitely a challenge to act like there was no communication. But I feel so fortunate that they allowed us to work together."

Getting Acquainted

Ken Kwapis designed exercises to help the actors get to know each other as real people — as well as in character. Alexis Bledel began filming in Santorini a full month before the other girls would start. The girls had been encouraged to e-mail each other, and they kept in touch.

"When Alexis was in Greece, we checked in and talked to her a lot," says Amber. "We hung out in Los Angeles before we actually left to start shooting the film. The process of being friends before the film started helped a lot."

After the shoot in Greece, Alexis joined her costars for a week of rehearsals in Vancouver. One of the rehearsal exercises was a shopping trip. Kwapis took the four girls to a vintage clothing store and gave them each some money. He asked them to buy something—in character.

While it may seem a strange way to rehearse, Kwapis watched the girls start to become their characters and, "more importantly, the group dynamic started to happen," he says. "It was fascinating." Over the course of several hours, some of the shoppers needed advice from others, while some gave too much advice. Later, Kwapis says it was interesting to talk about "not what they bought, but how the group functioned. Was Lena too afraid of Tibby's opinion? Why was Carmen the last one to buy anything? Could Bridget find anything in the store that suited her sporty character? And when she couldn't, who did she look to for advice?"

During another rehearsal, Kwapis took the girls to the yoga studio space where the Sisterhood's mothers meet in prenatal aerobics class. There, he told them he'd leave them alone for forty-five minutes. Just before locking the door, he warned, "You'll never have another opportunity again to be literally alone with no one but yourselves."

He worried about what they might do. "I thought, 'I better check back in forty-five minutes or they're going to be bored out of their minds.' So I went back in and they kicked me out! They said, 'Come back in another hour.' They loved it, but to this day, I don't know what they were doing."

Kwapis explains his intention. "So much of what I wanted to do was get these characters together and eavesdrop on them. The key to the picture was to create an atmosphere, and it's all by atmosphere that these actresses felt completely free. Everything else had to take a backseat to creating an atmosphere in which these young women felt uninhibited. Otherwise it's just people reading lines."

Music to His Ears

"I like to think of this film as a piece for four voices," he says. "Sometimes there's a polyphonic texture—when the four are stuck in the car together. And sometimes there's a duet or a round or a canon. The four voices together form the music of this picture."

Many of the crew members complimented the director on his endurance. "When the four were together," he recalls, "it was a bit cacophonous. But it was all by design. What was great about having all four of them together was to let them work themselves up into a frenzy of fun and friendship. Nothing made me happier than the fact that when the four girls were together, I didn't have to do much except stand back and turn the camera on and let them go."

Laughs and Chemistry

Alexis Bledel hadn't worked with people her age before. She says she "loved working with the other girls. It was really fun and we got along really well. We were all on the same page. To fake it would have been really hard to do. It's great luck that we like each other."

"There's a lot more energy, humor, and vivacity than I ever expected," says Denise Di Novi. "The chemistry between them is really electric."

"We have an organic chemistry," adds America Ferrera. "We just kind of hit it off. We had a lot of laughs and it was very easy to pretend to be friends."

"I'm so happy to have made the friendships I've made with these three girls," says Blake Lively. During filming, America attended one of Blake's choir performances. "We really had a support system."

Will they notice if I take this slice?

"There's a lot of times where it's really sweet and endearing, and there are lots of inside jokes. I think we've come up with probably more inside jokes than with any other friends I've ever had," Amber says with a laugh. "I felt so bad for Ken because sometimes he couldn't get our attention. We were just like chickens in the henhouse, yakking all the time. We're really lucky that the four of us have equally sick senses of humor."

"They were playing friends who have known each other sixteen years," says Kwapis. "The fact that they were so quickly able to develop their own inside jokes as actresses was great. Many crew members, especially the guys, would ask, 'How do you deal with this? They're so loud and they won't stop talking or they're talking on top of each other and nobody can understand a thing they're saying.' But for me, it was that kind of intense friendship, that's what it's like if you're in the middle of it. They understood each other perfectly."

We love this book!

Production Diary:
How We Made It Happen

by Christine Sacani, Line Producer

What Is a Line Producer?

My guess is that line producers are called that because they watch the bottom line—the budget—and they work on the line—on the set. The line producer gives the director everything he wants or needs to make his vision come alive onscreen, and does it within the parameters set by the budget. To do this job well, a line producer should be able to solve problems efficiently and with good humor.

On Location

If you've read the book, you know that <u>The Sisterhood of the Traveling Pants</u> takes place all over the world. Well, when you make a movie from a book, you don't usually have the option of going to every place in the book. Often you have to make it look as if you went somewhere even though, well, you didn't. Because of time and money, you just can't. In the case of <u>Sisterhood</u>, we had to narrow down the shooting locations to a manageable four places that would be "film friendly"—not necessarily film centers like Los Angeles or New York City, but places where we could get people and equipment in and out fairly easily.

We decided we could shoot the scenes set in Bethesda, Maryland, and Charleston, South Carolina, in one place—Vancouver, British Columbia. That left us with Greece and Baja to figure out. Greece was easy—no option there, we would have to go to Santorini, since there's nowhere else quite like it in the world. The Baja locale wasn't quite as simple to figure out, but eventually we settled on filming it in two places—British Columbia, Canada, and Cabo San Lucas, Mexico.

Setting the Schedule

Early in the process we discussed the order of countries for filming. It would seem natural to shoot the main location first, followed by the secondary locations. But for us, the decision was not so simple. Santorini is the number one tourist destination in Greece and the number seven tourist destination in the world. It would be tough to shoot there under normal circumstances—add the fact that the Olympics would be under way in Athens at the end of our schedule and our decision became clear. We would have to shoot Greece first.

Bonding Time, International Style

When a crew is away from home, the members are forced to form a new sort of family. We are with each other twenty-four hours a day, seven days a week, for better or worse. In Greece, in our case, it was for better. The bonds we created during the first two weeks of shooting were unique and lasted for the duration of the project. We truly did form a sisterhood (or brother-sisterhood, as the case may be).

Shooting a movie on an island in the middle of the Aegean Sea wasn't easy. But it was wonderful. Because

Cache Creek.

Santorini is not a film center, equipment and crew had to be brought in from other parts of the world. Our heads of department were flown in from Canada, the U.S., and England, while the secondary crew was brought in from Athens or hired locally in Santorini.

The Great North American Soccer Search

The second most difficult challenge location-wise was finding our Mexican soccer camp. After weeks of scouting all over Mexico for our perfect soccer camp, it was decided that our Mexican soccer camp wasn't there! The beach was there and it was beautiful, but the soccer ditch in the middle of the desert—as envisioned by our director —would have to be found (or created) somewhere else. Our search continued.

I remembered shooting a scene for another movie in a remote desertlike location in Canada, a place called Ashcroft, about an hour outside of Kamloops. As it turned out, our production manager had recently shot on a

ranch in Cache Creek, and we immediately sent for photos. The stars aligned and we planned a trip there the following weekend.

Turning the Desert Green

The location was beautiful. Our director, with the help of our production designer and visual effects supervisor, could "see" his soccer camp there, and we moved forward with the decision to film there—good news, since we'd be leaving for Greece to begin our preparation work in less than two weeks. That brought us to our next big challenge: growing green grass in the desert.

Here we were with a hundred construction guys and acres and acres of arid sand in the middle of the Mojave Desert. Heated discussions ensued about whether it could be done or whether it might be smarter to go with the traditional dirt soccer pitches that prevail in Mexico. The latter would prove rather dirty and difficult to pull off in its own right, plus it wouldn't give us the beautiful shock

Can we make grass grow? You betcha!

of green that was etched in the mind of our director—so green grass it would be. A plan was created to lay an underground watering system with tenting to protect the grass from the harsh summer sun and 110-degree mid-day temperatures.

And it worked! The guys took care of the grass as if it were an invaluable greenhouse full of rare orchids. And it was beautiful. No one wanted to put their cleats on it—but we did end up playing soccer there—and lots of it!

Can You Hear Me Now?

While we were shooting at the remote ranch, cell phone service was nearly impossible. There was only one place on the playing field where you could get reception—in front of Cabin 6 at five feet off the ground on the porch to the left of the front door. Otherwise you had to go a mile up the road, get loaded into the scissor-lift that we had waiting, and get lifted fifty feet in the air. Needless to say, both options proved quite frustrating during our five-day shoot there!

Hot Stuff

Imagine playing soccer all day long in 110-degree temperatures? Well, these girls did it! We cast the four soccer teams right there in nearby Kamloops. We got actual soccer teams that were used to the sweltering heat—thank goodness! I've never seen so much water and Gatorade be consumed in such a short time.

Shooting this film was a fantastic experience—and I hope everyone has as much fun watching the film as we had making it!

A Brief History of Pants

PART 3

The story continues. . . .

Tibby was playing back some footage she'd shot for the documentary she was making when the doorbell rang. Switching off the TV, she went to answer it.

A girl was standing there holding a FedEx package. "I think this is yours," she told Tibby. "They delivered it to my house by mistake. My name's Bailey—"

"You're the one who fainted," Tibby interrupted. "The other day at Wallman's. I was there."

Bailey nodded. "Oh, yeah. You were the weird girl with the price sticker on your forehead."

Tibby returned Bailey's red wallet. But instead of thanking her, Bailey accused her of stealing some of her money! So far, Tibby wasn't crazy about her young visitor. Bailey was sort of obnoxious.

Does this belong to you?

When her baby sister started to wail, Tibby hurried inside to comfort her. Bailey followed and started poking around in Tibby's video equipment.

"You making a movie or something?" she asked curiously. "Maybe you need an assistant."

"Maybe I don't," Tibby countered.

"You wouldn't have to pay me or anything," Bailey said eagerly. "I could just, you know, help you carry equipment and stuff."

Before Tibby could say thanks but no thanks, her mother came home. After saying hi, Bailey left. "See you round, Tibby," she said. *⁎

Weren't <u>we</u> supposed to play together?

Carmen and her father were on their way out of the house to play tennis when Lydia called to them.

"Darling, I've got to meet the caterers at the hotel. Would you mind stopping by Paul's game?" she asked Al.

Al agreed. To Carmen's dismay, she soon found herself sitting beside her father, watching her future stepbrother's soccer game.

"Which one is yours?" one of the other fathers asked Al.

"Paul," Al replied proudly. "Paul Rodman."

Just then Lydia raced toward the bleachers, calling Al's name and looking upset. It turned out that a water pipe had broken at the hotel where the wedding was supposed to take place.

Al hugged her as Paul wandered over to see what was happening. "Let's get you home and we'll figure this out," Al said. "Hey, Paul, how would you like to play tennis with Carmen?"

Soon Carmen and Paul were trading volleys at the local tennis club. Carmen couldn't believe that her father had done this to her. Paul barely spoke! She was so angry that she accidentally smashed the ball right into Paul's forehead. ✿

Bridget flirted with Eric every chance she got. But he didn't seem to be falling for it. His lack of interest might have discouraged some girls. But it just made Bridget more determined than ever.

Whenever she spotted Eric watching her team practice, she played even harder than usual. She was so focused that didn't notice how annoyed her coach, Karen, was getting until Karen pulled her from the field one day.

"This is a scrimmage, Vreeland," Karen said angrily. "We all know you're a superstar, okay? We got it. Now, save it for the championship."

Bridget was annoyed, but she didn't let it bother her for long. She had bigger things on her mind. Eric might pretend he wasn't watching her. But she could tell that he was.

Lena hoped she wouldn't run into Kostos when she went to return his shirt. But he arrived as she was trying to leave it on his boat. "Here's your shirt," she said. "Thanks again."

Kostos smiled at her. "They told you, didn't they?"

Lena was surprised at his expression. "You think it's funny? Our grandparents hate each other." But she realized this was her chance to find out more. "What's the fight about, anyway?"

"What everything here is about. Money and fish. My grandfather says your grandfather cheated him, and your grandfather says my grandfather sold him fish that made everyone in his restaurant sick."

"So what's the truth?" Lena asked.

Kostos gazed into her eyes. "The truth is, it's a beautiful day. Why should the rest of it matter?"

"Because it does." Lena turned and walked away.

Duncan was in a snit because Tibby had worn the Pants to work. "I'm afraid our dress code strictly prohibits blue jeans," he said testily.

Luckily, it was time for Tibby to leave. When she emerged from the store, she found Bailey waiting outside with her video equipment. Tibby's mother had let Bailey in to fetch it.

Tibby still didn't particularly want to be friends with this girl. But Bailey had already lined up an interview for Tibby's video. Tibby decided she might as well check it out. It seemed easier than trying to ditch her new "assistant."

Bailey led the way to the local convenience store and pointed out a boy playing a video game. "His name is Brian McBrian," she whispered. "King of the Quik-Mart Dragon Master. I hear he's broken every record there is."

Tibby couldn't help being impressed. Brian McBrian seemed to be the perfect loser subject for her "suckumentary."

They set about taping Brian playing his video game. He explained that he was the only player ever to make it to Round 28 on that machine.

Tibby found herself getting caught up in Brian's enthusiasm. Before she knew it, her camera was out of tape.

"We could always come back, I guess," she commented to Brian. "That okay with you?" *

He's perfect.

Carmen was feeling rebellious. She was sick of being stuck in the land of the Perfect Blond People. She tried speaking Spanish to her father, but he put a stop to it quickly, since the others couldn't understand her.

Then Lydia told Carmen the latest wedding news. They had decided to hold the whole thing right there at home. They all seemed really excited about it, but Carmen didn't share their feelings.

Suddenly she realized she hadn't seen Paul in quite a while. At first she was afraid that wild tennis ball to the head might have something to do with it. But her father pulled her aside to tell her the real story.

"He's in Atlanta, honey," he explained. "Visiting his father. His dad's in a rehab facility there—for alcoholism. Every month Paul takes the bus to visit him. Krista refuses to go—she isn't ready to see him."

Carmen was surprised. Maybe the Perfect Blond Family wasn't so perfect after all. ✿

Quiz: Which Pants Girl Are You?

Answer the following questions about life, love, and pants. Then check the answer key at the end to find out whether you're most like Bridget, Carmen, Lena, or Tibby . . . or a little of each.

Now, these are pants.

(1) If you had to pick one of the following to use as your life's motto, which would you choose?
(a) Always look on the bright side.
(b) Live and let live.
(c) Banzai!
(d) Life sucks, then you die.

(2) Which of the following animals do you identify with the most?
(a) A dog—everyone's best friend, loyal, smart, and beloved.
(b) A cat—a loner, an observer, but willing to snuggle and purr now and then.
(c) A cheetah, running wild, fast, strong, and free.
(d) A platypus. Just because.

(3) What's your favorite kind of pants?
  (a) Anything cute, colorful, and sorta slimming is cool by me.
  (b) No pants, thanks—I prefer skirts and dresses.
  (c) Jogging pants, shorts, khakis, jeans—whatever doesn't get in my way.
  (d) Who cares? Pants are pants. There are more important things to think about in the world.

(4) Which of the following features is most important to you in a significant other?
  (a) Smarts, kindness, a great sense of humor . . . I want it all!
  (b) Understanding. Without that, what's the point?
  (c) Anyone I hang with has gotta know how to have fun!
  (d) Honesty. Blunt, tactful, or somewhere in between, just tell me the truth, the whole truth, and nothing but.

(5) How do you usually approach a new experience?
  (a) I wouldn't say I like change, but I take it in stride. Or at least I try.
  (b) Avoidance, avoidance, avoidance.
  (c) Straight on, eyes wide open, and full steam ahead.
  (d) As a thrilling new opportunity for sarcasm.

(6) What's your favorite part of the school day?
  (a) Homeroom or between classes, when I get to catch up with my friends.
  (b) Art or music class, where I can express myself.
  (c) Gym class—I definitely prefer basketball to books.
  (d) Lunch. What better place to observe the rainbow of human dorkitude in all its glory?

(7) How are you with foreign languages?
  (a) I am bilingual or close to it.
  (b) I do my best but I'm nowhere near fluent.
  (c) The only language I care about is universal—body language.
  (d) I speak Geek and Dork fluently, and I'm well on my way to learning Loser.

(8) Which of the following attitudes best matches your own?
  (a) I am who I am—take me or leave me. But I hope you'll decide to take me. Please?
  (b) Look before you leap.
  (c) Leap before you look.
  (d) Live free or die.

Score Yourself

Turn each (a) answer into C for Carmen, (b) into L for Lena, (c) into B for Bridget, and (d) into T for Tibby. Now see how many of each initial you have.

✿ **Mostly Cs:** You are most like Carmen. Smart, optimistic, quick to laugh or cry, you're a loyal friend. It's great to be in touch with your emotions, but be careful not to take things too personally or let yourself be hurt too easily. Take care of yourself—after all, your friends are counting on you!

💕 **Mostly Ls:** You are most like quiet, artistic, observant Lena. You may be shy, but still waters run deep. Watch out that you don't go so deep inside yourself that you forget to reach out to other people. They have a lot to offer you— and vice versa.

I like it like that.

✯✯ **Mostly Bs:** You are most like outgoing, athletic Bridget. Treating life as one big adventure, you are bold and fearless; you know what you want, and you're not afraid to reach out and grab it. Just be sure it's what you *really* want.

✳✳ **Mostly Ts:** You are most like Tibby. Cynical, smart, probably a little sarcastic, you look for the cloud behind every silver lining and pride yourself on your honesty and clear view of the world. While it's good to be a realist, be careful not to get too gloomy. Life may suck, but it's the only life you have.

Half C, half L: You want to be everybody's friend, but you're not quite sure you dare. Sensitive and emotional, you're slow to trust but loyal once you do.

I've got to get out of here.

Half C, half B: You are the life of the party, outgoing and lovable. You'll do anything for a laugh or a good time, but you're also willing to stand up for a friend or any other worthy cause. You always know the right thing to say, and you aren't afraid to speak up.

Half C, half T: You are fiercely loyal to a chosen few . . . and who cares what the rest of the world thinks? You're unique, perhaps flamboyant—and proud to be one of a kind.

Half L, half B: You are the object of everyone's envy—you can do it all. But sometimes you feel like a big fake. Don't worry. You're not the only one who feels that way, no matter how much it may seem like it sometimes.

Half L, half T: You tend to be cautiously radical in thoughts, looks, and behavior. A free spirit, you sometimes wish you didn't have to deal with other people at all. But in the end, your natural curiosity leads you back to your favorite position as observer of the human circus.

Half B, half T: You do exactly as you want, and you don't care who objects. People might describe you politely as unique, or less politely as a freak. But who cares what other people think? Not you! Being like everyone else is boring!

A combo of all of the above: You are the perfect balance—what Carmen would call a complete person. That doesn't mean you're perfect—then again, maybe it does!

What just happened?

A Peek Behind the Scenes:
Film Trivia

I've got some sketches to show you.

Amaze your friends with these fun facts and
behind-the-scenes stories from the filming of
The Sisterhood of the Traveling Pants.

Piano Man

Did you happen to notice the man playing the piano at the ballet recital near the beginning of the film? No? Well, take a closer look — that nimble-fingered guy is actually the film's director, Ken Kwapis!

Is it worth the tape?

Tibby's Video

For Tibby's "suckumentary," Ken Kwapis was in charge of the Brian McBrian portions and the lemonade stand scenes. But actresses Amber Tamblyn and Jenna Boyd shot the rest on their own in and around Vancouver.

A Girl's (New) Best Friend

During filming in Vancouver, Blake Lively found and adopted an adorable stray dog. After that, the dog went everywhere (except Mexico) with her.

Pen Pals

It was important that the girls' friendship seem real onscreen. To help them get better acquainted, the film's dialogue and acting coach, Mary McCusker, had the girls keep diaries and write to each other as much as possible.

Emmy Girl

Amber Tamblyn was in Vancouver shooting *Sisterhood* when she found out she'd been nominated for an Emmy award for her work on *Joan of Arcadia*. The rest of the movie team helped her celebrate her achievement with an Emmy-shaped cake.

Untold Stories

The third assistant director in Greece, Dimitris, was so eager to please the director and get the best performances out of the background talent that he created full biographies and life histories for each and every extra in the film. For instance, all Lena's relatives had stories including how they were related to her, where they lived, their jobs, etc.—even though we never hear a word of it in the film. Talk about attention to detail!

Casting Kostos

After seeing the film, you may be wondering where they found that Greek heartthrob who plays Kostos. The filmmakers flew three candidates to Santorini to audition with Alexis Bledel—two from the United States and one from Athens. Which young actor got the part? If you guessed it was the boy from Athens, you're wrong. It was Michael Rady from Philadelphia!

Greek god or Philly boy? Either way, Michael Rady shines as Kostos.

Lena, disappointed that he didn't notice her, discreetly
repositions herself closer to the shop. She sneaks glances
into the fish market, watching Kostas sell his daily catch to   *
a merchant inside.

When Kostas emerges, she quickly returns to her drawing. He   *
walks right by her, strapping the ice chest back onto his
Vespa before finally acknowledging her.

                    KOSTAS   *
          Been here long?

                    LENA
               (feigning surprise)
          Kostas, what are you doing here?   *

                    KOSTAS   *
          This is one of the places I sell my
          fish.
               (beat)
          But you already knew that.

                    LENA
          Excuse me?

                    KOSTAS   *
               (grins at her)
          No one sits near a smelly fish
          market unless they're waiting for
          someone.

Embarrassed, flustered, Lena packs up her things to go.

                    LENA
          I don't know what you're talking
          about. I was just sketching that
          church over there.

Kostas moves to stop her from leaving.   *

                    KOSTAS   *
          Wait.
               (nods to her sketchpad)
          May I?

                    LENA
               (hesitates)
          It's not finished.

His hand remains held out to her, and Lena relents, giving
him the pad. He studies the sketch for a long moment.

In Their Own Words

PART 3

About the Book

The Sisterhood of the Traveling Pants by Ann Brashares was published by Delacorte Press, an imprint of Random House Children's Books, on September 11, 2001. It quickly became a worldwide bestseller, as did the two companion novels that followed, *The Second Summer of the Sisterhood* and *Girls in Pants: The Third Summer of the Sisterhood*. "We knew we had something very special with the book," says Wendy Loggia, editor of the *Sisterhood* books at Delacorte. "And to watch a book that we love so much be embraced by readers around the world and now become a major motion picture—it's beyond thrilling."

"It's a full emotional meal," says Debra Martin Chase of the novel. "It's about the power and beauty of friendship. It covers the whole gamut—the joy is intense, the emotion is real and heartfelt. You love the characters, you love the journey, and you love the magic of the Pants. From a cinematic standpoint, it has everything."

Denise Di Novi says the bestseller appeals to several generations because "the stories and the emotions are timeless. We all remember what it's like to be that age and face those challenges and dilemmas. All the characters are unique and what they deal with is so universal that it's really captivated people's imaginations and won their hearts."

From Page to Screen

"THE SISTERHOOD OF THE TRAVELING PANTS"

CUT 1/3 ④ — LENA SKETCHES
SC: ㉝ SHT: ②

CUT 1/3 ⑧ — LENA SKETCHES A SAILBOAT ANCHORED IN FRONT.
SC: ㉝ SHT: ③

CUT 1/3 Ⓒ — THE DUDE STARTS TO APPLY LOTION ON HIS (TOPLESS) GIRL-FRIENDS BACK.
SC: ㉝ SHT: ④

②

1/04

THE SISTERHOOD OF THE

CUT 1/6 ④ — SC: ㉝ EXT- SMALL HARBOUR (AMMOUDI)
SC: ㉝ SHT: ① CONT

CONT 1/6 ⑧ — ONE SHOT ... PAN → — RIGHT TO THE SEAWALL. LENA IS PERCHED DRAWING. WE PUSH IN AND ...
SC: ㉝ SHT: ①A CONT

CONT 1/6 Ⓒ — ... ARM DOWN
SC: ㉝ SHT: ①B

①

1/04

From Page to Screen

"THE SISTERHOOD OF THE TRAVELING PANTS"

(*) CONT'D FROM PG. (5)
(*) CONT'D FROM PG. (5)
(*) CONT'D FROM PG. (5)

(*) CONT'D FROM PG. (5) ...RIGHT TO SEE A WELL BUILT YOUNG MAN WORKING ON HIS NET.

...Dolly
SC: (33) SHT: (11A)

/A

/B

LENA'S EYES WIDEN.

SC: (33) SHT: (12)

/C

THE YOUNG MAN LOOKS BACK, SMILES, THEN DUCKS OUT OF FRAME.

SC: (33) SHT: (13)

/A

SC: (33) SHT: (1)

/B

+/LENA; SHE SKETCHES THE SEAGULL.

SC: (33) SHT: (10)

/C

THE SEAGULL POSES. WE DOLLY...

DOLLY...

(*) CONT'D ON PG. (6)

SC: (33) SHT: (11)

(*) CONT'D ON PG. (6)

(5)

1 /04

I've got to make room for these.

The novel was adapted for the screen by Delia Ephron and Elizabeth Chandler. Debra Martin Chase recalls Ephron's reaction after she read the novel. "Delia said, 'You need the ultimate summer romance in this movie. You've got everything else in here.'" Chase was thrilled. "She totally got what the movie should be—how to preserve the very best of the book but also make sure it was translated to the screen in the most effective manner." After several meetings, Ephron set off to write. "Her first draft came in and it was terrific," says Chase.

One of the biggest challenges in adapting the novel to the screen was its structure—"how to make the five stories connect in a way that felt natural, not jarring," explains Chase. "Several studios passed on the book specifically because of the structure—they were afraid of it."

One of the differences between the novel and the screenplay is that in the movie, the Pants go to each girl twice. "The first time they go around, each girl thinks the Pants have been a disaster," says Kwapis. "The Pants cause Lena to almost drown. For Tibby, the Pants don't do anything at all—they're mismailed. In Carmen's case, they cause her to throw a rock through a window and alienate her family. And for Bridget, they cause her to flout the rules at camp."

Sneaky. Sneaky.

But during the second go-round, the girls feel they can use the Pants. Kwapis compares the story to *The Wizard of Oz*. "The girls in the Sisterhood have all the things they need. They just don't know it."

In the novel, Lena and Kostos don't get together until the end—and their romance has her grandmother's full blessing. In the film, the ultimate summer romance is an opportunity for Lena to blossom—in spite of her grandparents' wish to keep them apart.

For the second draft, Elizabeth Chandler worked closely with Kwapis, "pinpointing very emotional moments in the book and trying to bring them to the screen. Each girl goes through a milestone; that's why it's such a huge summer," she says.

The author is pleased with the adaptation of her book. "It doesn't shy away from emotional and rich situations," says Brashares. "When people think about teenagers, they go for the most obvious and shallow stuff. That's unfair and doesn't properly represent that time of life at all. So I love the fact that the movie is really taking on some big stuff. And I think the spirit of the movie is pretty true to the book, or at least what I was trying to do with it."

Reading Along

During filming, almost everyone involved in the production read the novel. Amber Tamblyn was an exception. "That was a conscious choice," she explains. "A lot of times when there's a translation between a book and a script, things are taken out, and I didn't want to be disappointed." Amber wanted to focus on the character she was playing, as opposed to the one in the book. "I really wanted to know Tibby from the script. I love the screenplay for what it is and I like to think of it as a substory of the book," which she read once she'd completed filming.

"I thought the book was amazing," says Blake Lively. "Ann Brashares is so brilliant." She notes that while the script is quite loyal to the novel and "portrays the book beautifully, there [are] little differences, minor and major, that will keep fans of the book on their seats and still guessing."

America Ferrera adored the script and as soon as she landed the role of Carmen, ran out and bought the book. "I fell in love with it, and now I'm a fan, before anything else." When Brashares visited the set during filming, America talked the author into allowing her a sneak peek at the third book in the series, *Girls in Pants*, which wouldn't be published until January 2005. America spent every available second with the new novel, savoring every word.

What America enjoyed most about *The Sisterhood of the Traveling Pants* was that "it jumps off the page and reminds you of your own best friend. It felt so empowering to see girls really caring about other girls. And while it's a book for young girls, it talks to them at a mature level."

For girls only? Not according to Bradley Whitford, who plays Carmen's father. The actor admits, "I suffered the humiliation of crying in a coffee shop as I finished this book about these four girls."

The Meaning of Pants

Ann Brashares thinks jeans are the essential pants. "Integral to whether you look good is whether your pants fit. As ridiculous as it seems, it's something some of us spend a certain amount of time worrying about. I'm trying to get over that as I get older, three children later," she says with a smile.

"It's every woman's fantasy to find that perfect pair of jeans," says Debra Martin Chase.

"I think you view jeans with a judgmental quality," Brashares muses. "You have your skinny jeans, your fat jeans, your sexy jeans, and it's sort of like you allow them to judge you. For me, the Traveling Pants transcend because they're unconditional. They don't judge. They love these four girls equally. They fit all four of them, as differently built as they are. It's sort of taking this almost controversial, judgmental, restrictive piece of clothing and reforming it, so that the Pants are unconditionally loving and fit four different girls."

"The girls are tentative about being away from each other," adds Elizabeth Chandler. "The Pants are a touchstone and represent something to hold on to, to ground them, on their independent adventures."

photograph by Peter Freed

Ann Brashares.

A Brief History of Pants
PART 4

Meet me.

Lena sat sketching outside a fish market. When Kostos appeared she tried to play it cool, but he wasn't fooled. "No one sits near a smelly fish market unless they're waiting for someone," he said. Then he insisted on seeing what Lena was sketching. Shyly, she let him look, and they wound up having a deep conversation about art.

Then Kostos told her why he wasn't still living in Chicago. His parents had died in a car accident when he was seven.

Later Lena sat near a waterfall and wrote to Carmen: *Despite everything he's suffered, he can still look at life in the most uncomplicated way. People like Kostos and Bridget, who have lost everything, can still be open to love. While I, who've lost nothing, am not.*

The idea made her sad. It also made her feel strangely bold. Stripping to her underwear, she jumped into the pond and swam beneath the waterfall. She'd never done anything so impulsive in her life. It was exhilarating!

Where are nose plugs when I need them?

First love.

Then she heard someone move nearby. Kostos! At first Lena was embarrassed. But Kostos joined her in the water without a word. It felt right to be there with him, swimming and splashing and enjoying the moment.

That was the turning point. From that moment on, Lena and Kostos spent as much time as possible together, though Lena often felt guilty, knowing that her grandparents wouldn't approve.

Late one night they took his boat out into the harbor. Lena tried to explain why she'd been so aloof at first.

"It's all right, I understand." He brushed her hair from her face. "Some people show off their beauty because they want the world to see it. Others try to hide their beauty because they want the world to see something else." 💜💛

From Page to Screen

Leukemia?

Tibby was getting used to finding Bailey waiting for her every day when her shift ended. One day Bailey didn't show, and Tibby went to her house. A neighbor told her Bailey was in the hospital.

"She has leukemia," the neighbor said. "Found it a couple of years ago, poor thing."

Tibby was stunned.

She was interviewing some random losers the next day when Bailey found her. "Need some help?" Bailey asked.

"Yeah, sure, absolutely," Tibby said brightly, trying to hide what she knew. "It's good to see you, Bailey."

Bailey guessed right away that Tibby had found out about her disease. Feeling guilty, Tibby suggested they go find someone new to interview.

"Are you just asking 'cause you feel sorry for me?" Bailey demanded.

Tibby thought about it. "Maybe."

Bailey shrugged. "Okay."

They interviewed one of Tibby's coworkers. Tibby paid a lot more attention to Bailey than she ever had before.

Later Tibby and Bailey lay on their backs looking

More than meets the eye?

at the stars. Tibby finally worked up the nerve to ask the question she'd been wondering about ever since learning about Bailey's illness: "Are you scared?"

"Not of dying, really," Bailey said thoughtfully. "It's more that I'm afraid of . . . time. Not having enough of it, I mean. I'm afraid of what I'll miss." *⁎

From Page to Screen

Wish I had my car.

Bridget found out that Eric and the other counselors were going to the local cantina one night. She and her friends sneaked out and followed them there. Eric was surprised to see her.

"You shouldn't be here," he told her.

But Bridget laughingly dragged him onto the dance floor. She pulled out all her sexiest moves as they danced together. Eric was having a great time, but he forced himself to pull away.

"I can't do this," he said. Then he walked off the dance floor.

Bridget could tell he'd had enough for that night, but she didn't care. There would be other nights to change his mind. To convince him that she was worth a little risk.

Her first opportunity came soon afterward. She found him sitting on the beach one evening at sunset watching the waves. They talked for a while.

Nothing else happened that night. But Bridget knew she was making progress. ✦

I know you want me.

Carmen was trying to fit in with her new "family," but it wasn't easy. She didn't seem to have anything in common with them. Only one good thing happened around that time—the Pants arrived.

This one?

She wore them to the bridal shop where she was to be fitted with a bridesmaid's dress for the wedding. Lydia and Krista came, too. Krista loved her dress. But Carmen hated it on herself. She knew she looked ridiculous.

"Oh, dear," the tailor said disapprovingly. "I think we might be better off just starting from scratch on this one."

Carmen could only take so much. After a few more snide comments from the tailor, she took off the dress, pulled on the Pants, and stormed out of the shop. Lydia called after her, but Carmen didn't look back.

Hours later, Carmen took a taxi back to her father's house. She felt guilty about rushing off; she hoped Al and the others weren't too worried.

The house was quiet, and she figured everyone was out looking for her. She sat down on the porch to wait, but then she heard noises coming from inside. Walking around the corner of the house, she came to the dining room window—and froze.

They were in there. All of them. Al, Lydia, Paul, and Krista were sitting at the table eating dinner and chatting. As if nothing at all were wrong. As if Carmen weren't missing.

As if Carmen didn't exist.

Anger bubbled up inside her. Without stopping to think, she grabbed a rock and hurled it through the window with all her might. Then she turned and ran away.

From Page to Screen

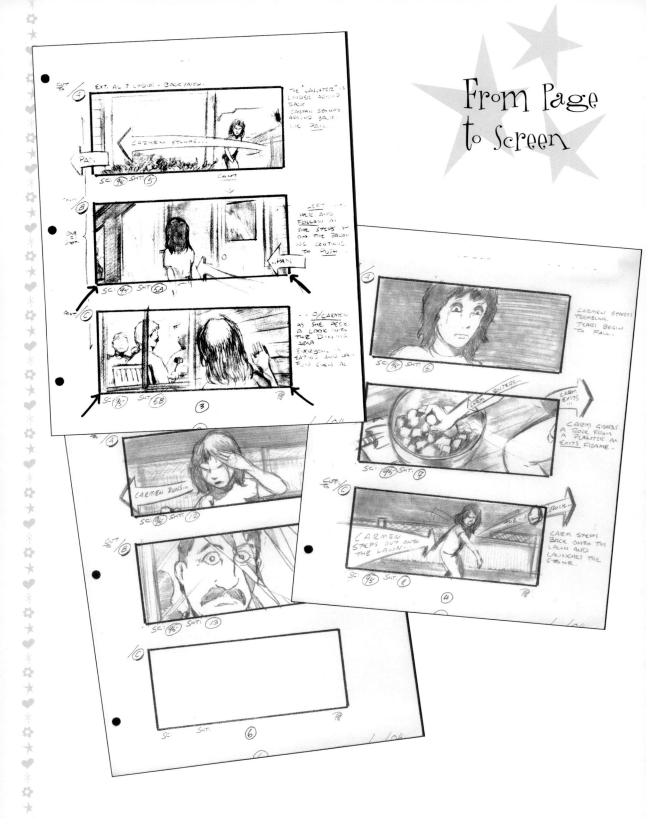

From Page to Screen

Carmen took the bus back to Bethesda without telling her father she was going. Back home, she got ready to send the Pants to Bridget.

Then Tibby came over to her house. Carmen told her friend what had happened in South Carolina. "It felt like I was living in some freak show known as the Land of the Blonds," she said bitterly. "And guess who was the freak."

"I'm sure they weren't that bad," Tibby said.

Carmen couldn't believe her friend was sticking up for them. She tried again to explain how horrible they were. But Tibby didn't seem that interested.

"Could you at least pretend to be on my side here?" Carmen exclaimed.

"This isn't about sides, Car," Tibby replied. "I'm just saying there are worse things than your dad getting married."

That wasn't what Carmen wanted to hear. Before she knew it, she was yelling at Tibby and calling her a hypocrite. She regretted it almost immediately, but she was still too mad to take it back. Without a word, Tibby got up and left the room. ❁

Bridget was excited when the Pants arrived. "Do you realize what this means?" she exclaimed.

Her bunk mates were confused. "That you're hugging a pair of jeans?" one of them said.

"They're not just jeans," Bridget corrected. "They make things happen."

That night as her bunk mates slept, Bridget pulled on the Pants and sneaked out. She went to Eric's cabin and peeked in the window. He was awake, and when he saw her he followed her outside.

And I'm gonna take full advantage.

"Did you know I would come?" Bridget asked him.

"No." Eric paused. "I hoped you would."

Later Bridget felt numb as she curled up on her bunk. How could something that was supposed to make her feel so complete end up leaving her so empty? She wished she could talk with her mom. But that could never be.

The next morning, her cabin mates asked her what had happened.

"Nothing," Bridget said, feeling too tired and confused to tell the truth. ⭐

A Peek Behind the Scenes:

The People Who Made It All Happen

It takes a village. . . .

A film is a labor of love shared by many people
working behind the scenes—director, writers, producers,
crew, and more. Here's your chance to get to know a
few of them a little better.

Ken Kwapis *Director*

Ken Kwapis's work has graced both big screen and small. His features range from the romantic comedy *He Said, She Said* (starring Kevin Bacon and Elizabeth Perkins) to the screwball comedy *Dunston Checks In* (starring Jason Alexander and Faye Dunaway). He made his feature film debut directing a man in a bird suit in *Sesame Street Presents: Follow That Bird*. The most ambitious television comedies of the past ten years—*The Larry Sanders Show, Freaks and Geeks, Malcolm in the Middle, The Bernie Mac Show,* and *The Office: An American Workplace*—were all also directed by Ken.

Debra Martin Chase *Producer*

An Academy Award– and Emmy-nominated motion picture and TV producer, Debra includes among her credits *The Princess Diaries* and *The Princess Diaries 2: Royal Engagement* and, on TV, Rodgers & Hammerstein's *Cinderella, The Cheetah Girls,* and the Lifetime series *Missing*. She began her career as an attorney, receiving a degree from Harvard Law School. In October 2003 *Essence* magazine named her one of the fifty African American women shaping the world.

Denise Di Novi *Producer*

Denise is considered one of Hollywood's top producers. Among the many films to her credit are *What a Girl Wants, A Walk to Remember, Heathers, Little Women, Catwoman, The Nightmare Before Christmas, Edward Scissorhands,* and *Batman Returns*. She began her career in journalism and eventually moved into the film industry as a unit publicist before rising to head her own production company.

Andrew A. Kosove and Broderick Johnson *Producers*

Andrew and Broderick are copresidents of Alcon Entertainment (Alcon is named after an ally of the mythological figure Hercules, an archer who never missed his target). Andrew and Broderick produced *Dude, Where's My Car?* and *Insomnia,* along with the family film favorites *My Dog Skip* and *Racing Stripes*.

Melissa Wiechmann *Co-producer*

For the past three years, Melissa has worked as Head of Development for Martin Chase Productions. She is also the co-creator/executive producer for Byou, the new fitness brand for girls.

Steven P. Wegner *Co-producer*

Steven is the Vice President of Development for Alcon Entertainment. He supervised the development of, co-conceived, and executive produced *Racing Stripes*. He also developed and co-produced *Love Don't Cost a Thing* and *Chasing Liberty* and was associate producer on *Insomnia*.

Christine Sacani Co-producer

Christine is a veteran producer of more than forty film and television productions, including co-producing *New York Minute*. With television as her foundation, she counts among her many accomplishments *Eloise at Christmastime* and *Eloise at the Plaza* and the musical drama *South Pacific*.

Alison GreenSpan Executive Producer

As President of Development for Di Novi Pictures, Alison helped develop the script for *The Sisterhood of the Traveling Pants* and helped oversee the film's production. In addition, Alison executive produced *New York Minute*, *What a Girl Wants*, *Eloise at the Plaza*, and *Eloise at Christmastime*.

Leslie Morgenstein Executive Producer

Leslie Morgenstein is the President of Alloy Entertainment and has overseen all phases of development and production of the company's properties, including *The Sisterhood of the Traveling Pants*, *Gossip Girl*, and *The A-List*.

Kira Davis Executive Producer

Kira serves as Vice President of Production and Marketing for Alcon Entertainment, where she's worked since 1997. During her tenure at Alcon, she has overseen the productions of *Lost & Found*, *My Dog Skip*, *The Affair of the Necklace*, *Love Don't Cost a Thing*, *Chasing Liberty*, and *Racing Stripes*.

Delia Ephron Screenwriter

Delia's screenwriting credits include *You've Got Mail* and *Michael*. Her next movie project is *Bewitched*, a film based on the popular TV show, which she is cowriting with her sister, Nora. Delia's new novel, *Franny 1000*, will be published in 2006.

Elizabeth Chandler Screenwriter

Elizabeth's screenwriting credits include *What a Girl Wants* and *Someone Like You*.

Ann Brashares

Ann Brashares grew up in Chevy Chase, Maryland, and attended Sidwell Friends, a Quaker school in the D.C. area. She studied philosophy at Barnard College, part of Columbia University. Ann took a year off after college to work as an editor, hoping to save money for graduate school. Loving her job, she never went to grad school, but instead worked as an editor for many years. Ann made the transition from editor to full-time writer with her first novel, *The Sisterhood of the Traveling Pants*, followed by *The Second Summer of the Sisterhood* and *Girls in Pants: The Third Summer of the Sisterhood*. All are *New York Times* bestsellers.

In Their Own Words

PART 4

Pants with character.

To find the all-important Pants, "We interviewed different jeans," producer Chase says with a smile. "In the end, a magical pair of Levi's was cast in the coveted role of the Traveling Pants. Jeans have become such a part of both fashion and everyday life. They have different personalities. We considered going with a hip, newer brand, and several were interested in being cast, but at the end of the day we felt there was something great about Levi's. They've been around forever, it's a great American brand, and there's something classically classical about Levi's. They never go out of style. They define what jean is all about. Finding a pair of Levi's at the vintage store evoked all kinds of possibilities of where they could have traveled to arrive here." The Traveling Pants are Levi's Super Low Cut Stretch Boot Leg.

Ann Brashares never specifies what brand the Traveling Pants are in the novel, but she happily notes, "I always envisioned them as a well-worn pair of Levi's—they couldn't have been better cast."

With the exception of being aged, the jeans appear unaltered in the movie. "It never happens that a costume is in the title," says costume designer Lisa Jensen. However, she points out, costumes were no more or less key in this film than they are in any story. "The magical Pants are supposed to be something that can be common to any girl. Like the problems that the girls have, everybody has problems, everybody has a life that they're trying to grow into, and these Pants, even though they're magical, they're something the girls can share."

Pants Magic?

Director Kwapis isn't choosing sides. "The four girls have everything they need already—the Pants are the agent that brings it out. Carmen *does* have the courage to face her father. Lean *does* have the ability to come out of her shell. Bridget *does* come to realize that the reason she pursues boys has nothing to do with sex but everything to do with grief, the loss of a parent, and the fact she is desperate for a man—and it's not Eric but her father that she needs. And with Tibby, it's a story about how she may be invested in her anger and the idea that everyone is leading lives of quiet desperation, but somehow inside there's a heart beating. When it comes time to step up, she goes to the hospital to visit the friend that she didn't want to have. All their problems are solved by themselves. So what did the Pants do? They allowed things to happen and they offered a springboard for the girls to do what they already could. They just didn't know it."

"It has nothing to do with pants," insists America Ferrera. "It has to do with the magic that the girls' relationship puts inside the Pants. When we hold the Pants and hug the Pants, we're not loving the Pants, we're loving each other. They wore these Pants, and now I have a piece of them with me."

"I like to think of these Pants as a true friend," Ann Brashares says, "in that they don't tell you what you want to hear. They don't make your life easier and more pleasant along the way. They force you into reality, into seeing life as it is and into sometimes doing hard things."

A Brief History of Pants
(the Regular Kind)

These days almost everyone wears pants and jeans without a second thought. But it wasn't always that way. Just fifty years ago, most women and girls never wore pants at all! Check out these historical pants moments and other trousers trivia.

Approx. 700 BC: Pants are worn by the Scythian, Dacian, and Sarmatian people.

Late fourth century AD: During the Roman Empire, pants are considered so offensive that an imperial decree fines people for wearing them.

1789: The start of the French Revolution. Working-class revolutionaries are known as "Sans-culottes" ("without knee breeches") because of their long, baggy pants.

1829: Loeb "Levi" Strauss is born in Bavaria.

1850s: Hoping to provide women with more freedom of movement, a feminist named Amelia Bloomer creates a new kind of outfit consisting of nearly-ankle-length skirts worn over long, full pants gathered at the ankles. However, these "bloomers" are widely ridiculed and soon disappear.

1864: The word *denim* appears in Webster's Dictionary.

1853: Levi Strauss moves from New York to San Francisco and starts a wholesale clothing business, supplying gold miners and others.

1872: Strauss makes the first copper-riveted "waist overalls" (aka jeans).

1890: Chicago engineer Whitcomb L. Judson invents the zipper.

Early 1900s: Some women start to wear split skirts (today known as culottes) so that they can ride bicycles. Many people condemn the style, and it never becomes popular.

1909: A Napoleonic law that bans women from wearing pants is lifted— but only for women who are "holding a bicycle or the reins of a horse."

1930s: Hollywood Westerns help to popularize denim jeans. Movie star Marlene Dietrich receives a warning from French police after appearing in public in a trouser suit.

1940s: American soldiers during World War II sometimes wear Levi Strauss's jeans while off-duty.

1950s: Many high schools forbid students to wear blue jeans.

1960s: Bell-bottoms become a favorite choice of the groovy generation. (They were originally created for sailors—the flared bottoms meant the wearer could remove his boots quickly in an emergency.)

1980s: Jeans become high fashion when designers Calvin Klein and Gloria Vanderbilt and others put their names on the back pockets of fashion victims across the USA.

2000 and beyond: Denim is everywhere. From celebrities with $300 pairs to soccer moms, babies, and teens, wearing jeans is always cool. And vintage jeans? Very cool. And pricey! Did you know that used Levi's can cost over $250 in Japan?

Famous Pants-Wearers in History

Katharine Hepburn: Born in 1907 and a movie star for most of her long life, Hepburn wore pants at a time when it was nearly unheard of for women to do so. Hollywood studio staff members once hid her pants, replacing them with a skirt—so Hepburn walked around the studio in her underwear until her pants were returned!

SpongeBob SquarePants: The lovable pants-wearing animated TV character premiered on Nickelodeon in 1999, giving a whole new angle to pants fashion.

The Ultimate Pants-Related Head-Scratcher

Why are pants referred to as pairs? The word *pants* is always plural, even when you're only referring to one item.

The truth is, the singular *pant* has been around since the late 1800s, but hardly anyone really uses it. The word *pants* was first recorded in 1840, an American slang term for *pantaloons*, a word that was itself first recorded around 1600 and has been variously applied to different types of garments.

But that doesn't really explain the plural thing. For that, it's necessary to look even farther back in history. Until the late 1600s, leg coverings consisted of two sleeves of fabric—one for each leg. These separate pieces were usually attached to a belt to keep them up.

So there you have it—a pair of pants!

In Their Own Words

PART 5

carmen's bedroom.

The Art of Creating the Look

When production designer Gae Buckley was sixteen, she had three best friends. "So I knew these girls. They were familiar to me," she says.

"Gae just so totally got the girls," says Debra Martin Chase. "She's done an amazing job with all our sets and location designs."

Buckley and her team worked with a specific color range for each main character. Lena was blue and white; Bridget was green.

"Carmen was bright red and rich pink and fuchsia," says Buckley, "so she would really stand out against the plainer color field of Al and Lydia. And Tibby's world was mini-malls, large stores, fluorescent lighting and colors unknown to nature."

In designing for the scenes in which the girls discover the Pants, Buckley recalls Debra Martin Chase's noting that she wanted it to feel as if you could find the magic anywhere. "We didn't want too much magic in the store, but we wanted to create a place that had the feel of a worn pair of jeans." To accomplish this, the art department let remnants of blue paint peek through the painted bricks.

The yoga studio needed to feel like a safe, warm environment. "I wanted to keep some of the pink," says Buckley, "because it was the place that, when you first meet the girls, they're literally in the womb. And the second time it's their heart center, where they go to create the bond of friendship."

This place has some special pants.

Lena's bedroom.

Dressing for Success

In designing costumes for *The Sisterhood of the Traveling Pants*, Lisa Jensen had to keep in mind that "all of the characters had to be kept very different from one another and still look like they were good friends. That mostly came from having strong personalities, as opposed to any fashion sense."

Jensen describes Lena as "poetic and delicate. I always thought her character was incredibly feminine, even though she tries to hide it." Lena's character undergoes the biggest wardrobe transformation. Her baggy skirts and endless layers give way to clothes that gently reveal her body. "But not too sexy," Jensen points out. "It's about feeling the air on her skin."

Carmen is colorful, "but not overly flamboyant," says Jensen. "She's not afraid of her curves, not embarrassed by the fullness of her body. That changes a bit when she goes to her dad's. But Carmen has a healthy sense of self. It's her heart and family she's struggling with."

Jensen didn't want to make Tibby Goth, but she needed what she describes as "another piece of the spectrum—in-your-face graphics, vintage and contemporary mixed up." Tibby wears heavy shoes "to make her clomp around so she'll make more noise than other people."

Bridget is classically contemporary. "She has a credit card and can go shopping," Jensen explains.

Carmen's desk.

Quiz: Where in the World . . . ?

The Traveling Pants wouldn't be what they are without, well, the traveling. Take this quiz to figure out which hot spot from the film is the best match for your own travels.

(1) **SCENERY: Which would you rather see out your window in the morning?**
   (a) Just give me a beach and some sun and I'm a happy camper.
   (b) Quaint old buildings, blooming magnolias, and horse-drawn carriages.
   (c) Gorgeous, exotic views of whitewashed walls, sparkling waves, and sunshine.
   (d) Who cares about morning scenery? I'd rather sleep in.

(2) **PEOPLE: Which of the following types would you like to encounter during your vacation?**
   (a) Laid-back and friendly with a fiesta flair.
   (b) Polite, soft-spoken, and normal.
   (c) The more different they are from me, the better. I don't even care if we don't speak the same language—that just makes things more interesting!
   (d) Who wants to deal with other people on vacation? Keep them all away from me!

(3) FOOD: Which of the following sounds like your ideal vacation dinner menu?
- (a) Stuffed clams, ceviche, and other *pescados y mariscos*.
- (b) Fried chicken or shrimp, corn bread or biscuits, and collard greens.
- (c) Spanakopita, tzatziki, pseftokeftedes, kalamari, and baklava.
- (d) I like to keep my diet simple. Just give me the same food I always eat.

(4) ACTIVITIES: How do you like to spend your time on vacation?
- (a) Swimming, sports, and soaking up the sun.
- (b) Sightseeing and relaxing.
- (c) Sightseeing, trying new things, and learning about other cultures.
- (d) Sleeping and watching TV.

(5) DISTANCE: Pick the statement you agree with most from the list below.
- (a) I don't mind a little travel if it's going to get me somewhere interesting, but I get restless if I have to sit still too long. I want to spend my time enjoying my vacation, not getting there!
- (b) Travel to foreign lands is fine in theory, but I'd rather see the USA first.
- (c) I'm willing to travel any distance, by plane, train, or automobile, to get to somewhere exciting and new. The world is my oyster!
- (d) Why waste time and energy traveling? Wherever you go, there you are. So why not stay home?

Mexico.

Add up your answers and see where in the world you should go.

Mostly As: Pack your bags—you're going to Baja! You can make like a beach bum, enjoying the sand, sun, and surf—but with just enough of the exotic to satisfy your adventurous side.

Mostly Bs: Charleston, South Carolina, is the destination for y'all. Oozing with Southern charm, this sleepy little city is sure to win your heart.

Mostly Cs: Better get your passport ready, because you're off to Santorini, Greece! While there, you can explore the narrow, twisting streets, meet the charming natives, taste delicious local specialties—even gaze out over the caldera of a volcano!

Mostly Ds: Your preference is to stay put, whether you're in Maryland, like Tibby and the gang, or a different spot. Vacation, schmacation . . . in your opinion, there's no place like home!

carmen's casa.

It's All Greek to Me

It didn't take long after arriving in Santorini for Lena to realize that her Greek wasn't quite up to par. Carmen didn't really need her fluent Spanish in South Carolina, though Bridget probably could have used her help in Baja. If you're planning to make like the Pants and travel, it helps to speak the language of wherever you're going. Start preparing yourself to see the world by learning these useful words and phrases.

English: *pants*
Greek: *panteloni*
Spanish: *pantalones*
French: *pantalon*
German: *Hosen*
Italian: *pantaloni*

English: *good-bye*
Greek: *andio*
Spanish: *adiós*
French: *au revoir*
German: *auf Wiedersehen*
Italian: *arrivederci*

English: *hello*
Greek: *yasoo*
Spanish: *hola*
French: *bonjour*
German: *guten Tag*
Italian: *ciao*

English: *friendship*
Greek: *filia*
Spanish: *amistad*
French: *amitié*
German: *Freundschaft*
Italian: *amicizia*

English: *thank you*
Greek: *efharisto*
Spanish: *gracias*
French: *merci*
German: *danke*
Italian: *grazie*

Production Diary: Stunt Coordinating Takes On a Whole New Meaning

by Lauro Chartrand, Stunt Coordinator

Can I rest for one Second?

What Is a Stunt Coordinator?

The person responsible for overseeing all the physical action in the film's production: training the actors and stunt performers so they are physically and mentally ready to perform the stunt action required, communicating with the director and producers, organizing and casting all the stunt performers, securing and setting up the proper equipment to make the stunts work safely and correctly, and, most importantly, seeing that the proper safety precautions are taken to keep all performers and crew as safe as possible. Not to mention donkey wrangling.

Quick Decisions and Lost Luggage

It all started with a surprise phone call from line producer Chris Sacani asking if I could read the script and come in and meet with Ken the next morning. Before you know it, I was off to Athens. I arrived in fine shape—but unfortunately my luggage did not accompany me. While reporting this to the airline I met a lovely lady who was going through the same situation as I was, and who just happened to be one of our producers, Debra Martin Chase.

After shopping for new clothes and toiletries, I spent a couple of days in Athens trying to help Ken with some of the local casting. It was important for the actors to have the proper skills for some of the roles, especially since we didn't want to use stunt doubles. Stunt people are a pretty rare commodity in Greece.

A Different Kind of Transportation Trouble

We were looking for three women to ride a Vespa motor scooter at one time. They were known as the Three Busty Cousins in the script. This apparently meant something else to the Greek casting team—they brought in a bunch of men!

Once we got that straightened out, we felt it would be best if the "cousins" had some previous riding experience on a Vespa. I was told not to worry, that everyone in Greece can ride a Vespa. I had hoped to audition a few women in Athens, but we had to leave for Santorini before it could happen. On the island, we saw three women for the role, two locals and one from Athens. The girl from Athens was the one who supposedly knew how to ride. But she was so stressed after trying to ride with the other two that she quit the next day!

Don't fall off, don't fall off . . .

With two days to go, we had to find someone who could ride a Vespa. The person we found couldn't really ride, either, but she was willing to try. We managed the scene by having the trio coast down the alley without the motor running. Since we were on a pretty good slope, they got up to a believable speed that way. And it worked out just as funny as we'd hoped.

Teaching our leading lady Alexis to ride a Vespa was actually pretty easy once we got her confidence up. The trouble was, the one Ken picked out was an antique—it was very heavy and always wanted to tip over. Even our leading man Michael had a bit of a struggle with it. Every time Alexis stopped, it tipped. Without having her lift weights for three months prior to filming, there was no way she would be able to manage it. So in the scene where she is learning to ride, we had the Vespa running but

Michael is actually pushing it and holding it up while she steers. Once again we got lucky and it came off looking great.

Donkeys!

Alexis and George ("Papou") had to ride sidesaddle on packsaddles, on donkeys, up and down very steep steps. Alexis was a little nervous, but she caught on great—even the part when she had to fall off!

How many more times do we have to do this?

Next came the shooting days of donkeys and extras and extreme heat. Not to mention donkey wranglers with no experience who didn't speak English (and even their Greek was questionable). Walter, our first assistant director, was getting a little anxious to get things moving along. So who became the official donkey wrangler? Yours truly! "Lauro, can you turn the donkeys around? Can you bring them over here? Can you get them to move faster?" However, I drew the line at picking up the nice little souvenirs they left on the steps from time to time!

It takes a lot of people to get a donkey down the stairs.

Dealing with problems is just part of the job. The whole experience was a great team effort and a lot of fun. It was an experience I will never forget.

In Their Own Words
Part 6

Shooting in paradise, aka Santorini.

It All Started in Santorini....

Lena's story is a real-life fairy tale. She meets an amazingly handsome, charming young man who is smitten and falls in love with her. He seems to understand her almost better than she understands herself. "It's that really great terrific first love that everybody dreams of, and we all hope we'll find," says Debra Martin Chase.

Alexis Bledel loved Greece. "It was fun; I'd never been there before." She describes Santorini as "really beautiful and relaxing. We went just before tourist season. A lot of the time it didn't feel like work—because of the ocean, which we could see from every part of the island, and the sunsets. It was great."

While the crew worked incredibly hard, "We did take moments to enjoy the profound physical beauty and spirituality of the place," says Chase.

However beautiful Santorini is, it is not a popular film location. And while the filmmakers were delighted to bring the exotic beauty of the island to an audience, Chase recalls wondering if

It looks like a postcard—but it's real!

there was a reason why movie crews avoided the location. "But much to our delight, the crews were great and the people were so excited about having an American movie shooting there. They could not have been more gracious or helpful, and it was a terrific experience."

"We wanted the audience to experience what the characters experience," says Denise Di Novi. "Santorini was one of the most beautiful locations I've ever shot in."

The Suckumentary

Abandoned for the summer in Bethesda, Tibby sets out to make what she calls a suckumentary, a documentary that reveals how everyone is leading lives of quiet desperation, because, says Amber Tamblyn, Tibby believes that "people are losers and have no lives."

Tibby's plans are foiled when she meets a young girl, Bailey, played by Jenna Boyd. Twelve-year-old Bailey insists on working with Tibby on the documentary, and along the way she shows Tibby what life is all about. As Tibby attempts to portray her subjects as sad and pathetic, Bailey finds endearing, positive qualities in them all. It becomes a battle for the soul of the documentary they're shooting.

To help prepare for their roles, Ken Kwapis wanted Amber and Jenna to actually shoot their own documentary. The director explains, "I didn't need to see it or know what they were doing. They just needed to do it in character."

Amber did the filming while young Jenna learned all about operating a boom microphone and sound mixer. Their equipment in hand, the girls set off, in character and without the director, to interview random people. "We tried to find people who could be

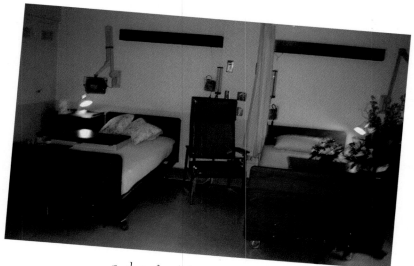

Bailey's hospital room on the set.

classified as 'loser,'" says Amber, "and the more I talked to people, whether it was a garbage man or a guy taking care of an island and shooting the rats for a living, I found these people to be really dedicated to their jobs and living very fulfilled, complex, amazing lives."

Kwapis explains that the rehearsal was a chance for the actresses to define themselves in opposition to one another. "It was a way for two people to look at the same thing and come up with the most diametrically opposed points of view."

Jenna's character, Bailey, suffers from leukemia. As part of her research for the role, she participated in a five-kilometer run to benefit the British Columbia Children's Hospital. There she met with staff from the hospital who work with children who have leukemia, and she also talked with young patients in remission about their experiences.

Five Stories in Three Countries

The Sisterhood of the Traveling Pants recounts four different summer adventures, one for each of the main characters. Add to that the narrative of the four girls together, and the movie tells five different tales.

When he first read the script, Kwapis imagined a film of contrasting values—"The great sun of Mexico, the antiseptic suburbia of Charleston, the overwhelmingly horrible, consumer-filled world that Tibby works in, and the breathtaking sensuality of Greece. How could these four environments fit in the same film?" the director wondered. "On the one hand, four wildly different characters, and yet a sense of continuity based on the fact that they're apart. Their sixteen-year friendship is the glue that holds them and the four stories together. There's never a moment when you're with one girl when you're not aware that they're thinking about each other. They're all in communication with each other on a spiritual level."

"This is a movie about four girls, without special effects," says Chase, "but from a production standpoint, we quickly realized we were making five movies and intertwining them in three countries. Everybody believed in this movie and gave two hundred percent and they worked tirelessly. And we had lots of fun!"

With sixty-eight locations, production designer Gae Buckley had her hands full. "It seemed like the company was almost always shooting two or three locations a day. We were out prepping another six to nine locations, plus opening the company every day. It was a puzzle of a time trying to get everything done."

To remember me by . . .

Four Parts = One Whole

"One of the challenges was giving each of the four stories a particular look but making them feel like they belonged to the same film," says Kwapis. The director had worked previously with cinematographer John Bailey.

"What I love about working with John is that we both have an appreciation of the classical Hollywood cinema," Kwapis says.

Wider-angle lenses were used on Santorini to make the environment seem more overwhelming. In Mexico, longer lenses were used to show Bridget setting herself apart from the crowd. With Carmen, shots were composed to reflect the awkwardness she feels. "A lot of the comedy in that story comes from the fact that she doesn't fit in visually," says Kwapis. For Tibby, to help express the edginess of her personality, "at times we'd get the camera off the tripod and shoot it in a more jittery way. Hopefully all these things have added up to a picture in which there's a complete sense of all the parts so distinctive that they add up to a very harmonious whole."

Bridget leans against her window, looking completely
different from the girl who came to Baja six weeks ago. It's
as if all the life has gone out of her.

CUT TO:

138   INT. TIBBY'S BEDROOM - DAY

Tibby sits on her bed, staring at her video equipment and
thinking about her promise to Bailey. Slowly she gets up and
walks to the array of videotapes assembled on her desk.
As she begins to sort through them, she comes upon one which
gives her pause. The label on it merely says "B." Puzzled,   *
Tibby pops the tape into the machine.

ON TV MONITOR

Bailey appears, seated on a stool and dressed in the Pants.
It's the interview she video-taped of herself that day.

                    BAILEY (ON TV)
              Hi, it's me. Bailey. Just wanted
              to see what it was like being on
              this side of the camera. You don't
              have to use it in your movie, or
              anything. Although now that I
              think about it, fainting in
              Wallman's does sorta qualify me as   *
              a loser.
                    (beat)
              Then again, wearing a price sticker
              on your forehead probably makes you
              one, too.

Tibby allows herself a small smile at this.

                    BAILEY (ON TV)
              I don't know, Tibby. Maybe the
              truth is, there is a little bit of
              the pathetic in all of us, you
              know?... Maybe happiness isn't
              about having everything in your
              life be perfect. Maybe it's about
              stringing together all the little
              things... Like learning a new
              skateboard trick, or wearing these
              Pants, or getting to another level
              of Dragon Master... And making them
              count for more than the bad stuff.

Tibby's eyes well up.

Bailey looks at the camera, smiling faintly as she utters:

A Peek Behind the Scenes:

You Think This Stuff Is Easy?!?

stay afloat!

Working on a movie might sound like a dream job—
and most of the people who made _Sisterhood_ happen would
probably agree that it is. But that doesn't mean
everything always goes smoothly.

Mexican Undertow

When you see Bridget and Eric jogging along the gorgeous Baja beach, it might look like a great place to hang out and go for a swim. But in reality, the water at that particular Mexican beach was so rough that the producers wouldn't let Blake swim in it.

Sink or Swim

There's so much salt in the Aegean Sea that it makes you float like a balloon. That made it so difficult to shoot Lena's drowning scene that they actually had to weigh her down! Naturally, there were safety divers nearby at all times to help her when she needed it.

Bridget Is a Hit

In the scenes when the girls are young, you may recall the moment when Bridget leaps off the ballet stage and takes a swing at one of the little boys laughing at Lena. During the filming of that moment, the little boy must have gotten tired of being smacked in take after take—in one take he actually hits her back! (That one didn't make it into the film, of course.)

Tiny dancers.

Bad Donkey Behavior

Did you ever hear the expression "stubborn as a mule"? Well, mules have nothing over the donkeys used in the film when it comes to stubbornness! The crew had to use six look-alike donkeys just to get the few minutes of donkey footage that appears in the film. One donkey was used for the walking parts. Another was pretty good at going *up* the steps. But a different one had to be used for going *down* the steps. And so on. (And according to the producers, none of them would ever hit their marks!)

Isn't Chocolate a Vegetable?

According to the line producer's assistant, Rudy Darden, during the filming of the running scene on the beach in Mexico, Blake and Mike craved Snickers. It was Rudy's job to locate these north-of-the-border sweets in the small Mexican town of Todos Santos. No word as to where he actually managed to find them.

Playing Catch-up

Before filming *Sisterhood*, Blake had never played soccer before. She had to train for three weeks to learn the basics so she would look like she knew what she was doing. She worked with a trainer in Los Angeles and, later, a soccer coach in Vancouver, who taught her the moves you see in the film. Because the soccer scenes were shot toward the end of the production, Blake had to keep up the running and training throughout the rest of the filming. That's one good way to force yourself to stay in shape!

Come On In

Think the water in Greece is always warm? Think again! The water was so cold during filming that Alexis and Michael were reluctant to jump in for their big rescue scene. To show them that it wasn't that bad, director Ken Kwapis stripped down to his bathing suit and dove right in. It was freezing . . . but he didn't let anyone see that he was the least bit cold!

Film crews always follow me when I run!

By the Numbers

11	Number of nationalities that worked on the film—American, Australian, Canadian, English, Greek, Mexican, Italian, Turkish, Scottish, New Zealander, Albanian.
50	Number of physical training sessions among Alexis, Amber, America, and Blake.
15	Number of days of soccer rehearsals for "Bridget."
2	Approximate weeks of soccer rehearsals for the rest of the soccer players, who were cast in Kamloops, British Columbia.
2	Approximate hours of driving the team to and from the set each day for the soccer players.
5	Number of tennis lessons for "Carmen."
2	Number of dance rehearsals for the cantina dance scene.
65	Number of cast members with speaking roles.
1,090	Number of extras (nonspeaking background parts).
11	Number of main-unit shooting days in Greece.
29	Number of main-unit shooting days in Vancouver.
5	Number of main-unit shooting days in Cache Creek, British Columbia.
4	Number of main-unit shooting days in Mexico.
1	Number of days lost because film was destroyed in the lab (Mexico).
312,640	Number of feet of film shot during the production.
429	Approximate number of airline tickets required during the production.
7,000	Approximate number of hotel nights required during the production.
450+	Number of crew members (not including postproduction crew).
6	Number of donkeys used in filming to play one donkey.

A Brief History of Pants

PART 5

Beautiful carma.

In a local taverna, Lena and Kostos slow-danced to the music of a live band. They knew it was one of the last evenings they would spend together; Kostos was leaving for school the following Monday.

"I love you, Lena," Kostos said, pulling her close.

Lena was filled with all sorts of emotions. She hesitated, trying to gather the courage to respond. Before she could, there was a commotion at the door.

It was Lena's grandparents. Papou strode over and pulled Kostos away from Lena, screaming at him in Greek.

"No, please!" Lena cried as Yia-Yia and her cousins grabbed her. Within seconds it seemed that everyone was shouting. Fights broke out, and Kostos could only call Lena's name in despair as her family dragged her away.

Later, Yia-Yia chided Lena. "You made promise to me," she said. "Does it mean nothing to break the hearts of those who love you?"

Lena was devastated by her grandmother's anger. As Yia-Yia strode out of the room, Lena fell on her bed, sobbing. 💜💙

In any language, this spells trouble.

Tibby was waiting for Bailey outside Wallman's when her mother drove up. "Bailey's in the hospital," Tibby's mom said. "She wanted you to know. If you want, I can drive you over to see her."

Tibby shook her head. "That's okay. I'll go by later, if I have time."

Later Carmen came over. Tibby ignored her at first, still angry about their fight. But Carmen started talking anyway.

"I'm mad at my dad," she said, sitting down on Tibby's bed.

That had been obvious to Tibby for a long time. "I know," she said coldly.

"Why is it so hard to say that?" Carmen wondered. "I have no trouble being mad at you." She apologized for the fight, and finally Tibby softened.

"Maybe it's easier to get angry at the people you trust," she said. "Because you know they'll love you anyway."

Once that was settled, Carmen asked Tibby about Bailey. "Is she going to be okay?"

"I don't know," Tibby replied. "I don't know."

Lena was sweeping the patio when the package arrived. It was the Pants.

She put them on, taking strength from all they meant to her. Then she went to talk to her grandparents. She told Papou she'd just realized how much alike the two of them were.

"Quiet and proud," she said. "Afraid of showing too much. And then I met someone who changed all that. You had the same moment once. When you met Yia-Yia. And you risked everything for it. For her."

When she put it that way, her grandparents finally started to understand how much Kostos meant to her. "Go," Papou said as Yia-Yia smiled.

Lena flew out the door, rushing down the hill to the ferry landing. She was just in time to catch Kostos preparing to board.

Kostos dropped his bags and rushed to her. They collided, falling into each other's arms.

"I thought I'd never see you again!" Kostos cried.

Lena gazed up at him. Finally she could utter the words in her heart.

"I love you." ❤❤

With Tibby there to encourage her, Carmen finally called her father. She could hear the hustle and bustle of the last-minute wedding preparations in the background.

He was happy to hear from her and eager to smooth over their problems. But Carmen knew it was more important to tell him what she was really feeling.

"I'm angry with you," she said. "This whole thing with Lydia and the kids . . ."

She went on, the words pouring out of her. She explained how the visit had made her feel like an outsider in her own father's life. How that made her feel as if she weren't good enough for him.

Eventually she broke out in sobs. "Why do you seem so happy about being Paul and Krista's father when you never had time to be mine?"

Al was silent for a long moment. "I'm sorry," he said at last. "I'm so sorry, honey."

Carmen could tell he meant it. But his words didn't fill the emptiness inside her. "I wish that was enough," she said softly before hanging up.

Letting it all out.

Meanwhile, Tibby still hadn't dared to think too much about Bailey. She ignored phone messages from Bailey's mother asking her to come to the hospital. If she didn't react to any of this, maybe it wouldn't be true. . . .

And at camp, Bridget wasn't acting much like her usual self. She messed up on the field, losing the championship game. But she didn't even care. ✿

When Tibby arrived home from her next shift at Wallman's, she discovered that the Pants had just arrived. She opened the package and read Lena's note.

These Pants are magic, Lena had written. *And I know if you let them, they'll bring you some, too. . . .*

That gave Tibby an idea. She took the Pants and went to the hospital. When she entered Bailey's room, the younger girl smiled weakly.

Making the most of time.

"'Bout time you showed up," she said.

"I brought you something." Tibby put the Pants on Bailey's bed.

Bailey touched them. "The Traveling Pants," she said.

Tibby explained what Lena had written about the Pants' magic. "So, I thought, well, maybe you could keep them for a while."

She stayed with Bailey for a long time. They looked out the window at the stars and talked.

Finally Tibby went home. She lay on her bed and looked out her window. When the phone rang, she heard her mother answering it.

A moment later her mother knocked on her door. "Tibby?" Her face and voice were solemn. "Honey—"

"I know." Tibby didn't want to make her mother say it out loud. Keeping her eyes on the stars, she nodded. "It's okay. I know." *⁎⁎

It felt strange to be home. Bridget couldn't seem to find any energy as she carried her bags into her house. She headed straight upstairs to take a nap.

The sound of crinkling paper woke her. Tibby and Carmen were there, unpacking piles of junk food. "See?" Tibby told Carmen. "I told you the smell of junk food would wake her up."

"I just feel so tired," Bridget told them.

Tibby and Carmen climbed into bed with her. "Talk to us, Bee," Carmen said earnestly. "Tell us what happened and we'll fix it."

Later, after a lot of serious talking—and eating—the girls lay groaning and full on the floor. Bridget's dog, Maggie, wandered in and spied the Pants draped on the bed. With a bark, she grabbed them and ran out of the room.

"Maggie, no!" Bridget raced after her. "Get back here! I mean it!"

She followed Maggie outside and down the street. Rounding a corner, she suddenly stopped dead. Maggie had stopped right in front of a very familiar young man.

"Eric?" Bridget was stunned. "What are you doing here?"

No Way.

From Page
to Screen

Eric was on his way back to Columbia. But he'd wanted to find Bridget and apologize for what had happened between them. "I never stopped to think that you might not be ready," he said. "Friends?"

"Friends." As they hugged, Bridget felt better. Talking to her friends had helped. So had seeing Eric again. For the first time, she figured maybe things would turn out okay after all. ★

Carmen, Tibby, and Bridget met Lena at the airport. When she sauntered through the gate wearing a casual yet sexy outfit, their jaws dropped.

Lena shrieked with joy and raced to greet them. "Oh, you're here! You're all here!" She hugged them within an inch of their lives. "I wasn't sure you'd be here," she told Carmen. "I thought you might have changed your mind about going to your dad's wedding."

Carmen pursed her lips. "No."

"Which is why we decided to change it for her," Bridget announced.

Tibby grinned at Lena. "You up for a little road trip?"

Carmen tried to protest. She thought her father should be the one to call and try to make her come to the wedding. "I was honest about all of it, and now it's his turn," she pointed out angrily. "Why shouldn't he be the one trying to fix it?"

Bridget shrugged. "Because as much as we think they're supposed to, parents don't know everything."

Tibby agreed. "The guy isn't perfect, Car. You can either accept that and choose to be a part of his life, or go on hating him for being flawed and miss out on having a dad."

Carmen saw their point. But she still wasn't totally convinced.

"What if he stops the wedding and throws me out?"

Her three friends exchanged glances. "We'll be there for you," Lena answered for all of them.

Courtesy of Bridget's new driver's license, they were soon in Charleston. They stopped in a diner to change clothes. Carmen was nervous, but her friends made her put on the Pants. They might not be the most appropriate thing to wear to a wedding, but they made her feel a little braver.

The four of them entered Al's backyard without being noticed and sat in the back row of chairs. Moments later the music started and Krista and Lydia walked down the aisle to join Al and Paul in front of the minister.

Just then Al spotted Carmen. As the minister began to speak, Al interrupted. "I'm sorry, could you just hold that thought? There's a very important member of this family who should be up here with us. My daughter. Carmen."

Carmen was overwhelmed. "But—I'm not dressed right. I look like I belong in—"

"You belong with us," Al insisted with a smile.

Carmen rushed up to hug her father. Suddenly everything was okay again. To her surprise, Lydia and the others seemed happy to see her, too. Almost as if they were a real family.

As Carmen said later, "It would be easy to say that the Pants changed everything that summer. But looking back now, I see that our lives changed because they had to. And that the real magic of the Pants was in bearing witness to this, and in somehow holding us together when it seemed like nothing would ever be the same again."

Some things never would be the same. But the four members

of the Sisterhood of the Traveling Pants knew that no matter how far they traveled on their own separate paths, somehow they would always find their way back to one another. And with that, they could get through anything.

They summed it up in a toast back in that deserted aerobics studio:

"To us," Bridget said. "Who we were, and who we are. And who we'll be."

"To the Pants," Tibby added.

"And the Sisterhood," Lena put in.

Carmen joined in. "And this moment, and this summer, and the rest of our lives."

In unison, they all spoke the final words: "Together and apart."

Together at last.